I0685035

DUSTY AYRES AND HIS BATTLE BIRDS:
BLACK LIGHTNING!

BLACK LIGHTNING!

By Robert Sidney Bowen

ALTUS PRESS • 2017

© 2017 Steeger Properties, LLC, under license to Altus Press • First Edition—2017

EDITED AND DESIGNED BY

Matthew Moring

PUBLISHING HISTORY

"Black Lightning" originally appeared in the July, 1934 (Vol. 5, No. 4) issue of *Dusty Ayres and his Battle Birds* magazine. Copyright 2017 by Steeger Properties, LLC. All rights reserved.

ALL RIGHTS RESERVED

No part of this book may be reproduced or utilized in any form or by any means, electronic or mechanical, without permission in writing from the publisher.

This edition has been marked via subtle changes, so anyone who reprints from this collection is committing a violation of copyright.

Visit ALTUSPRESS.COM for more books like this.

Printed in the United States of America.

CHAPTER 1
THE BLACK INVADERS

A FIST pounding against the other side of the door punctuated the shouted words. "Captain Ayres! It's important!"

The five-foot-eleven of bone and muscle stirred under the blankets, then sat up and blinked sleepily at the dark room. The fist pounded again on the door. With a grunt, Dusty slid out of bed, went over to the door and jerked it open.

A red-faced orderly clicked to attention and snapped a salute.

"The major's compliments, Captain," he said. "You are wanted immediately at his office."

"Right," nodded Dusty. "Be there in two shakes of a lamb's tail. Thanks."

Less than five minutes later the tall pilot shouldered into the office of Major Blake, C.O. of High Speed Group No. 7, U.S. Air Force.

"You want me, sir?"

The big man seated behind the paper-littered desk nodded and stood up. In his hand he held a folded sheet of paper. With a quick gesture he sailed it across the desk.

"You're elected, Ayres," he grinned. "Read it."

Dusty spread it out and looked at the teletyped message.

To Commanding Officer
High Speed Group No. 7—Dayton Field

1

Detail best pilot and plane for emergency courier work. Pilot will report to Room 19 War Department at once.

Signed, X34

As Dusty read it, the blood raced through his veins. He glanced questioningly at his superior.

"X34?" he gasped. "That's Chief of Intelligence, Washington, isn't it, Major?"

The other nodded.

"Right. And if you ask me, Ayres, this is your big moment. A big moment for all of us, I guess. It means that we'll soon get a chance to shoot at something besides tow-targets. In short—it means war!"

War! The word caught Dusty off guard, sent a strange eerie sensation tingling down his spine. War! To be sure, he'd expected it. As a matter of fact the whole country had been expecting war. It was inevitable.

Three thousand miles away a steel fist was pounding against the gates of Paris; battering to smoldering ruins the last European stronghold against ravaging hordes that sought to annihilate the civilized world.

For three long years all Asia and Europe had been a seething inferno of war; a war started by one man, a man of mystery. Who he was, or from whence he came, no one knew. But like magic he had risen up from an obscure part of Central Asia

3

and screamed his doctrine of eternal vengeance for all forms of government oppression.

The words had come not from his lips, but from the lips of unnamed agents, and the spark of unrest that flickered in the souls of the uneducated millions in that part of the world was fanned into a great white flame.

Almost overnight civil war and rebellion belched out from the vortex of hell itself, and consumed all it touched.

Nations tottered and fell, and were swallowed up by the great black wave that swept westward. The Black Invaders they became known as, and the man of mystery who commanded them they called "Fire-Eyes," the Emperor of the World.

The name was because of his eyes. They were like blazing pools of flame that looked out from behind a close-fitting green mask. Millions had seen him; his form-fitting black uniform, with no markings of rank save green-gold shoulder straps. They had also seen the black gauntlets that he wore, and the black spun skull cap that came down in the back to cover the nape of his neck.

Yes, millions had seen him, and even heard his harsh, cruel voice that could speak every language on the face of the globe, and speak it without a single trace of any other language.

But his true identity was a secret that no one knew. Those who had tried to find out died. Cruel, yet fearless, a maniac, yet a genius in leadership, he crushed the leading nations of two continents, bent them to his will, and molded them into his own great war machine.

And now, he was smashing the last European stronghold. If

4

he succeeded, the path across the Atlantic to America would be open. War—bound to come.

Dusty glanced at the Washington dispatch, and took a deep breath. Bound to come? Hell, that message meant that it had arrived, and that the United States Government was not going to be caught napping. He looked the major straight in the eye, and saluted.

"Thank you, sir, for detailing me," he said. "I'll do my best." The other nodded.

"I know you will, Ayres," he smiled. "Of course, this may mean nothing. But I don't think so. I think that you're going to be given a real job to handle. In case we don't meet again for a while, good luck, son."

As Dusty took the hand extended to him a queer feeling surged through him. A feeling that he couldn't exactly understand—as though something mysterious were waiting for him out there in the darkness.

He had a sudden crazy desire to laugh. Hell, he was letting his imagination do tricks. After all, he was simply going to do emergency courier work. The Black Invaders were three thousand miles away. Yet—

He shrugged, clicked his heels again and went outside and over to the hangar line. Floodlights sunk into the field turned the take-off runway into day. In front of the third hangar a plane was being dollied around, nose to the field. Its sleek body and taper wings glistened like silver.

A thrill of wild joy surged through Dusty as he ran over to it. What a ship! What a ship! The very last word in high-speed design. Fluted steel from prop to tail, chrome-dural wings with Presto cooling radiators in the top leading edge, and under the cowled nose, twenty-five hundred horses.

The Barling XFB she was known as officially, but to Dusty and his pals she was the Silver Flash. He'd painted the name on the nose, and just three days ago, at the group christening, he hung up an unofficial world speed record of 527 m.p.h. And that wasn't her top, either. He was certain that with a little adjusting he could add another 50 m.p.h.

The Silver Flash, the first one turned out. All his—and a special detail awaiting him in Washington. Boy, was he lucky and how! War? Okay, let her rip!

HIS HEART pounding with excitement, he legged into the cockpit and slid the glass cowling hood into place. With his finger he snapped on the ignition, and kicked the starter. Gears hummed softly for a second or two and then, with a loud click, the prop turned over. Two minutes later he shoved the throttle all the way home and braced himself.

Like a racehorse leaving the starting gate, the Silver Flash leaped forward. Its wheels seemed hardly to touch the runway, and before the second floodlight slid by, the plane was clear of the ground and streaking straight up into the heavens.

Eyes glued to the wind direction and speed indicator, Dusty gave the ship its nose. At thirty thousand feet he got the tail wind he wanted, leveled off, and set his robot control for a due east course. Then, slouching back against the headrest, he reached up and slid the glass hood open and adjusted his oxygen mouthpiece. The icy cool air of night whipped in at him and set the blood to tingling through his veins.

But suddenly he stiffened, sat bolt upright and closed the cockpit hood. A red eye on the two-way radio panel on the instrument board was winking rapidly. It was a signal that some ground station was trying to contact his wave-length.

Slipping the earphones over his head, he snapped up the "All Ready" switch and leaned toward the cockpit microphone.

"Captain Ayres, High Speed Group No. Seven, speaking."

As he switched over to the receiver the earphones made a crackling sound. And then to his utter amazement, a soft, purring voice spoke.

"My guns are trained on you, Captain. Change your course to due north, or I will shoot!"

Dusty gaped wide-eyed at the mike.

"What?" he blurted out. "Say, who are you?"

"A man who will kill you, if you do not obey at once," came the reply. "Change to north, and stand by for orders when to land."

Icy fingers ran up and down the back of Dusty's neck. In a quick movement he snapped off the cockpit light and strained his eyes at the black heavens. He was not sure, but he thought he saw something move above him and to his right. A split second later the voice spoke in the earphones again.

"I'm waiting, Captain Ayres. Fly north at once."

As the last word died away a tiny stream of sparks sliced across the dark sky, and Dusty heard the twang of bullets ricocheting off the steel side of the fuselage.

"Just a warning, Captain," said the strange voice. "The next will be through the glass hood over your head."

For one mad second Dusty sat frozen to the seat. Then, reaching out his hand, he switched off the robot control and took the stick. Gently he started to bank toward the north.

But when he had made a quarter of the turn, he suddenly thumped down hard on left rudder and pulled the control stick all the way back to his stomach. The Silver Flash shuddered, then whipped over and went down in a wild power spin. Instantly singing bullets twanged against the outside of the plane. But seconds later they died off and stopped altogether.

Lips pressed tight, eyes agape, Dusty held the ship in its terrific spin for a full ten thousand feet. His head was whirling, and there was an empty feeling in the pit of his stomach, but he hung on grimly until the altimeter needle registered twenty thousand feet. When it did, he braced himself, jerked the plane out of the spin and sent it streaking due east.

Shoving back the glass hood, he half raised himself from the seat and stared upward into the night. But he saw nothing but inky darkness. There wasn't even a moving blur that might be his mysterious attacker. And when he glanced at the radio panel he saw that the red light was no longer winking. That meant that the other had tuned off his wave-length. Brows furrowed, Dusty slumped back on the seat and stared dully at the instrument board. A thousand questions raced through his brain. What in hell was it all about? That tramp had tried to smack him down. And if it hadn't been for the Silver Flash's greater speed, death would have nailed him. But why? Who in hell could that other pilot be? How did he know Dusty was up here? And how the hell did he know his wave-length?

As reaction set in, the Yank pilot had a sudden desire to turn back, hunt out the mysterious attacker and give him a dose of his own medicine. And with the Silver Flash he could do it, too. The twin Browning guns mounted forward could spew death at the rate of fifteen-hundred shots a minute for each gun.

But he curbed the thought even as it came to him. He had his orders to obey. He flung one last look upward.

"Maybe some other time, you bum!" he grated.

THE WHOLE thing still rankled in his brain when an hour later he tore down out of the night and coasted to a perfect landing on the military field at Washington. As he taxied up to the hangar line and legged out, a field orderly ran over.

"Captain Ayres?"

Dusty nodded.

"Over here, sir," said the orderly, pointing to a waiting government car. "I'm to drive you to the War Department at once."

Dusty simply nodded again, and followed the man over to the car.

"Guess it's our turn next, huh, Captain?" grunted the orderly as he meshed gears.

"I guess it is," replied Dusty absently.

"Sure, sir. But it ain't going to be no cinch for them Black Invaders," went on the man. "That guy Fire-Eyes is going to have plenty of trouble licking a country a couple of thousand miles away 'cross the water. No, sir, he won't find a bunch of sorties like that European Army either. Funny how he wrapped them up so easy, isn't it, sir? But a pal of mine was saying that he done it by sorta busting up the country before he attacked them. You know, secret agents and all that kind of thing. They blow up reservoirs, and ammo and supply dumps. You know, all at once, like he did in Germany. And then it's a walk-over for him, because—"

But Dusty wasn't listening. A new thought had come crashing through his brain. The orderly had spoken about secret agents. Hell, that mysterious attacker could have shot him down without warning. Instead, he had ordered him to fly north and land. Why?

Well, it was a wild guess, but a possible one. The Silver Flash was the fastest thing in war aircraft. Neither the European Army nor the Black Invaders, themselves, had anything that could touch it. And it was the only one of its kind. Was some secret agent of the Black Invaders trying to get hold of it?

"Right, sir. This is it."

The orderly's voice jerked Dusty back from his reverie. The car was sliding in to the curb in front of the War Department building. As it stopped, the pilot jumped out and ran up the long flight of stone steps. A sentry at the door saluted smartly and held the door open. An elevator took him to the nineteenth floor.

Room 19 was at the far end of the hall. He paused in front of it a moment, glanced at the gold lettering on the glass.

General Horner

Chief of Intelligence

He knocked and entered. A thin lieutenant, seated behind a desk, scowled up at him.

"Who are you?" the officer snapped. "What do you want?"

Dusty gave him a leveled eye.

"Captain Ayres, H.S. Group Seven, reporting on orders."

The other's attitude changed instantly. His face lighted up with a look of respect, and his lips parted in a smile.

"Oh, Captain Ayres, the speed ace!" he exclaimed. "Yes, yes, Captain, you're expected. You'll find the general in the radio control room on the roof. Go right up."

With a nod, Dusty left the room and took an express elevator to the roof, forty-one stories higher. He stepped out into a great, glass-domed hallway. A soldier immediately confronted him, took his name and disappeared through a steel door. Dusty cooled his heels for a couple of minutes, and then the soldier reappeared. The man nodded.

"Go in, Captain," he said. "Fourth room on the right."

Returning the salute, Dusty went through the door, down the short hall to the fourth door. His knock brought a gruff summons to enter. As he did, a big officer standing back to him turned and studied him intently from beneath shaggy eyebrows.

"Yes, you're Captain Ayres," the officer suddenly boomed. "I'm General Horner. Sit down, Ayres."

Dusty obeyed and waited expectantly. But the general didn't go on speaking. Brows furrowed, hands folded behind his back the big officer fell to pacing up and down the length of the small room. Presently he stopped dead, turned and pointed a thick finger at the pilot.

"Captain Ayres, are you afraid to die?"

Dusty gulped.

"Why—why no, sir," he stammered. "I—well I really hadn't thought about it, sir."

"Well, think about it now," the general snapped. "Because, Captain, I'm going to detail you to a mission that may mean death. In fact, I'm going to place in your hands something that may prove to be the immediate safety of these United States of America."

The pilot slowly stood up, put his shoulders back, and looked at the general straight in the eye.

"I'm through thinking, sir," he said evenly. "I'm waiting for orders."

"Very well, then," nodded the general. "Now sit down and listen carefully. In case you haven't heard, the Black Invaders took Paris two hours ago. Right now the European Army—what's left of it—is in full retreat toward the French coast. That means we're next. Just when, I don't know. But for weeks, agents of this maniac warlord, Fire-Eyes, have been slipping into the country. A conservative estimate would put the number around ten thousand. That's what the easing up of the immigration laws five years ago has done for us."

The senior officer paused long enough to drop his big frame into a chair.

"WHERE AND how we will be attacked, I don't know," he went on presently. "Part of the Black Invaders' Pacific fleet is

concentrated somewhere off the Aleutian Islands. There's another couple of squadrons near the West Indies. The main part is off the French Coast. And that section will be doubled in size once Fire-Eyes captures the European Army fleet. Now, with his battle squadrons, airplane carriers, and fast transports so arranged in the waters about us, he can attack any part of our coastline within twenty-four hours after he gets steam up. Those cursed agents of his have pinpointed every one of our defenses. They know our strength to man and gun in every section of the country. Therefore, this Fire-Eyes has only to select a point of attack and arm himself in accordance with the defense he knows he can expect at that particular point of attack. Do you follow me, Ayres?"

Dusty nodded.

"I think I do, sir," he said. "You mean that his knowing our sectional defense strength robs us of any surprise defense in the event of an attack?"

"Right, Ayres. As things stand now, he knows what to expect from us, but we don't know what to expect from him. However, we've got a trick up our sleeves, and that's where you come in. Now listen, the general staff has worked out a last-minute mobilization plan. A plan whereby, during the twenty-four hours grace we'll have before the attack, we can shift our entire defense all around. Thus, once we do learn the point of attack, we will be able to concentrate on its defense. As a matter of fact, we've worked out several plans. But only one man knows which will be used. I am that man."

With surprising ease and speed for one of his bulk, General Horner slid out of his chair and came over close to Dusty. When he spoke, his voice was little more than a hushed whisper.

"Watch the second finger of my right hand, Ayres."

Dusty looked down at the hand. It was half buried in the palm of the left. Then the second finger moved, and tapped the left palm seven times.

"Make sure, Ayres!" came the soft command. "I'll repeat."

The pilot nodded and counted the seven finger taps again.

"Right, sir," he said. "I—"

"Shut up, Ayres!" the other hissed. "Listen to me first. That is the number of the mobilization plan to be used. I order you to guard it with your life, understand? Beginning with now, no one is your friend, see? You are to trust no one. You are to disobey every single order that you may get after you leave this room. Once my agent sends word that the Black Invaders have started toward our shores, you will take your plane and deliver that number by word of mouth to the commanders of the regional Army Corps areas. There are ten of them. You know their H.Q. locations, of course?"

"Oh, yes, sir. It was our job to contact them all, in those Air Force maneuvers of two months ago."

"Good, then. Their H.Q. locations are the same. And in order that they won't miss you, coded orders have already been sent out for them to stand by for your arrival. Now, everything clear? Any questions?"

Dusty pursed his lips, frowned slightly at the floor.

"I believe I understand, sir," he said. "But I'd like to ask a question, if you don't mind, sir."

"What is it?"

"Well, sir," began Dusty slowly, "even with my ship, it will take at least twelve hours for me to contact the ten corps area commanders. Why not transmit the secret number by short wave code, and save that much time?"

General Horner shook his head vigorously.

"Can't risk it, Ayres!" he said decisively. "For one thing, I suspect that the agents of the Black Invaders know every one of our short wave codes. Another thing, a circuit of secret transmitter stations in this country, that we haven't been able to smoke out yet, can clamp down on their high-powered transformers and jam the air. In fact, blanket out everything from the Mississippi valley to the Atlantic seaboard. That would put half our corps area commanders in ignorance of what they should do. No, Ayres, the only thing that they cannot do is pry words out of a man's brain. You can tap around wires, and air waves, but not a man's brain!"

The senior officer paused significantly.

"I mean just that, Ayres," he continued a moment later. "Nothing in the world can make a brave man speak, if he doesn't want to. But don't take this thing lightly. From this moment on, you travel with death. Guard that number. Contact the corps area commanders, no matter what happens. It is your one and only assignment until completed. Nothing else matters. Understand?"

Dusty nodded stiffly, started to speak, but checked himself as there came a sharp rap on the door. A red-faced staff captain entered. He didn't even bother to salute.

"We lost contact with Agent 10, sir!" he announced breathlessly. "I think they got him. His last message was blotted out."

For a second General Horner seemed stunned. Then frank disbelief spread over his face. He grabbed the staff captain by the shoulders, shook him roughly.

"You're crazy, man!" he roared. "Agent 10 was the one man we depended on. He's got to get word through to us!"

The captain paled and shook his head sadly.

"I know, sir," he said lamely. "But we haven't been able to raise his call signal for twenty minutes."

The general stared dully at the opposite wall and a low moan akin to that of some wounded animal rolled off his lips.

CHAPTER 2
YOU ARE NEXT, AMERICA!

IN SILENCE Dusty watched him. Suddenly the general shouted an exclamation.

"By God, there's just one chance!" he boomed. "The Telerad! Captain, get Major Jordon. Send him to me in the receiving room at once. Get going!"

As the staff officer bobbed his head and ducked out through the door, Horner turned to Dusty.

"Perhaps I've just been wasting my breath with you, Ayres," he said heavily. "God knows what may happen, with Agent 10 gone. But come along with me, and stick close, anyway."

With that, the senior officer started out of the room. Dusty followed at his heels. As they walked down a steel-lined corridor, disappointment swept over the pilot.

Five minutes ago he represented something really important in the welfare of the American nation. He had been selected to act as a key man in the great crisis to come. And now maybe Horner had been wasting his breath. Hell!

With a savage gesture, Dusty banished the thought. Damn it, important or unimportant, it didn't matter. He was an airman, the high-speed ace of Uncle Sam's brood, and it was his sworn duty to take what came and do the job as best he could, regardless of its degree of importance.

And so, head up, shoulders back, and a look of grim resoluteness on his wind-bronzed face, he followed the general through a series of rooms until they reached a large one that flanked almost the entire north side of the huge, glassed-over roof.

It was dimly lighted, and its four walls were lined with laminated strips of copper and steel, evenly spaced. Three sides of the room were covered with countless dialed instruments, each one fitted with its own tiny cowled light. And it was from these that the rest of the room got its light.

The fourth wall, however, was bare save for a framed square

of silver cloth, exactly in the center. General Horner started questioning a lieutenant who was bent over a teletype machine set against the south wall.

"You've tried everything, Gleason?" he asked harshly. "How about our emergency signal to him?"

"Everything failed, sir," replied the other gloomily. "Here's the last we got from him."

He handed the senior officer a strip of teletype tape. As the general straightened it out, Dusty saw the printed words:

10 TO INT. HQ... PARIS IS NOW A CITY OF DEAD AND DYING. IMPOSSIBLE TO ESTIMATE CASUAL-TIES. BLACKS IN FULL CONTROL AND PUSHING RETREATING EUROPEAN FORCES TOWARD FRENCH COAST. FIRE-EYES REPORTED TO HAVE LEFT IN HIGH SPEED BOMBER FOR... REPORTED LEFT... REPORTED... FOR... LEFT... LEFT....

"You see the ending, sir?" came the lieutenant's voice. "It just blotted out on the machine. All I could get was oscillating repetition. All call-backs failed. I'm afraid, sir, that—"

"I know!" groaned the general. "God, that man's a devil! My ten best foreign agents trapped and swallowed up in less than a week. Wait a minute, lieutenant. How about contacting European Army H.Q. direct? You know their emergency wavelength?"

For answer, the lieutenant pointed a finger at one of the dials. The indicator needle was stuck fast against the zero peg.

"Their station hasn't registered receiving power for over two hours, sir," he said hopelessly. "That means either that they've dismantled it and we'll be able to get through to them as soon as they establish the new station, or else their old station was captured and destroyed."

The general's mouth sagged down at the corners, and his eyes went dull.

"God, what a devilish mess!" he muttered. "I shouldn't have counted so much on Agent 10. Poor devil!"

HANDS LOCKED behind his back, the man started pacing slowly up and down the room. Dusty watched him with fascinated awe. Horner seemed like a man in a trance. His eyes were glassy, and the tiny blue veins at his temples stood out like taut cords. As he paced by Dusty for the tenth or eleventh time, the pilot put out his hand impulsively.

"Sir," he said helplessly, "is there anything I can do?"

The general stopped dead, and stared at him as though he were seeing him for the first time.

"Do?" he echoed thickly. "No, Ayres, there's nothing that any of us can do right now—except the Telerad. Hell, I'd been staking everything on Agent 10. I—he—well, he's been with the Black Invaders for over three months. Right in their midst, mind you, and keeping me informed of every move. He was our hidden ace. My—one of my own men, right close to this Fire-Eyes. It was Agent 10 who was going to send warning as soon as the Black Invaders headed for these shores so that we could make our last-minute preparations. God, I wish I hadn't— no, no, I'm proud of him. Damn proud!"

The general stopped with a husky cough. Dusty glanced at

the framed square of silver cloth in the center of the bare wall, hesitated a second or two, then took the bit in his teeth.

"Pardon, sir," he began, "but that thing up there. What—?"

The pilot didn't finish. General Horner was no longer paying attention to him. A signal unit major had come bursting through the door. The general grabbed him.

"Jordan!" he boomed, "it's up to you. We've lost contact with our one remaining foreign agent. We've got to get Williams at Brest on the Telerad."

The signal major nodded.

"I will, if he's there, sir," he said. "Our final experimental tests two weeks ago were perfect. I saw him clearly, and his voice came in okay."

"Then get to work!" Horner cried. "Never mind anything else. Get Williams, or God help us! We'll be a nation in the dark, waiting for the lightning to strike!"

The general shouted the last at thin air. The signal unit officer was already spinning dials and rheostat knobs at one end of the room. His hands worked so fast that it seemed he had a hundred instead of just two.

A high-keyed hum filled the room. It mounted and mounted until it faded off into nothing. The instant it stopped, Major Jordon clipped a transmitter speaking tube about his neck, and taking up a position in front of a foot-square switch board, he started flipping down a series of relay switches and jamming contact plugs into their sockets.

Then his lips moved, and Dusty heard his voice. It was measured and distinct in tone. But strangely enough, it did not seem to come from his lips. It was coming from a point in back of the framed square of silver cloth.

"Jordon 48, calling Brest 624! Jordon 48, calling Brest 624. Can you hear me, Brest? Can you hear me Brest? Oscillator set at 72. Jordon 48, calling Brest 624..."

On and on the man spoke, repeating every word at least ten times. Suddenly he stopped. Dusty, his eyes riveted to the square of silver cloth, sucked in a stifled gasp. Thin lines of rippling light were beginning to slide across its surface from left to right. Faster and faster they went, until they seemed to be traveling not only from left to right, but from top to bottom as well. And they made sound—a sort of soft hissing sound.

Presently the sound died out, and the lines of rippling light speeded up so that they all merged together into what looked, to Dusty, like a solid sheet of white flame. And then from its center came sharp clicking noises, and a split second later, the sound of a human voice.

"Williams at Brest, switching in. Your dial setting not true, 48. Swing to 7-2-0-1. Oscillator too high, 48. Swing to—check! You are registering! Send report on your end, 48."

As the last died away to the echo, the Telerad screen darkened a bit, and became shadowy in spots. The shadows spun in crazy circles, then suddenly ceased motion, and took on definite shapes with definite outlines. The head and shoulders of a thin American officer appeared on the screen. He was sitting in a chair, transmitter to his lips, and his hands were hovering over a dial board set at a slant in front of him.

"By God, he did it!" Dusty heard Horner breathe fiercely. "That's Williams at Brest. Oh, thank God!"

But Dusty wasn't listening any more. His body rigid, his lungs hardly daring to suck in a breath, he stood as a man of stone watching the figure on the Telerad screen.

It looked more like a ghost than a human being. The face was thin, sunken at the cheeks, and there was at least a week's growth of stubble on the man's chin. But it was his eyes that sent an icy chill slicing about Dusty's heart. They were like the eyes of a dead man—glazed and dull, as though they had looked upon things that the brain behind them could not forget.

No more than a split second for impressions of what he saw, and then Dusty heard Major Jordon's voice.

"Check, Brest… perfect. Stand by… emergency… X34 taking over this end… stand by."

WITH A quick wave of his hand the signal unit officer motioned Horner over, clipped the transmitter tube about his neck, and stepped back from the switch board.

The man at the Brest Station spoke almost at the same instant.

"Check, 48… registration perfect… go ahead."

Horner's voice boomed out from behind the screen.

"The latest, Brest. Give us the latest, at once. Agent contact completely lost. What's happening?"

"Black Invaders here on the coast," came the reply. "Retreating Europeans bombed and gassed to complete destruction. None of their units were able to retreat by water. Atlantic fleet of Blacks closed in on the coast. There is no hope for the Europeans. Their forces have collapsed completely. Black Invaders have control of all armament and supplies."

"But their next move, Brest?" Horner cut in. "When can we expect an attack? Where have the Blacks established their high command H.Q.?"

The man on the Telerad screen gestured and shook his head.

"I don't know. Bombing and transport squadrons have passed over here for the last hour, heading north by west. Possibly they intend to establish a remobilization base in England. The destruction of the retreating European Army was accomplished by gas bombers and high-speed mobile tank units under junior commanders. As yet, not a Black staff officer has been sighted in this area. My opinion is that the main part of the Black army is concentrating elsewhere for an immediate attack on America. I think—Oh, God!"

The man on the screen suddenly started clawing at his eyes and throat. His tongue welled up and pried his jaws apart, and the skin of his face and hands turned a hideous yellowish purple.

Choked, gurgling sound came from his mouth, and his body writhed in mortal agony. Then suddenly he toppled off the chair and disappeared from view.

Horrified, no one in that control room atop the War Department building uttered a sound. Like statues of stone they stood, staring wide-eyed at the Telerad screen. Then suddenly, Horner's thundering voice crashed against the terrible silence.

"Look! Look!"

There was no need for him to have spoken. They all saw the tall figure in black, with a green mask over its face, slide into

Williams' chair. And they all saw the inhuman, terrible flaming orbs of Fire-Eyes, the mysterious warlord of the Black Invaders—two pools of seething flame spewing out at them from behind the slits in the mask.

A second later his voice whipped against their eardrums. It was harsh, rasping, like tempered steel being dragged across jagged glass.

"Yes, look, America! It is me you see. Fire-Eyes, the Emperor of the World!"

Crashing laughter punctuated the last word.

"And you wish to know my plans, do you?" the masked figure continued. "Yes, I'm talking to you, X34—you, General Horner, chief of America's intelligence department! The time has come for me to speak to you direct. Take this message to your President, and your Congressional Committee for national emergencies. Tell them that the fate of your country rests with their compliance with my demands. And here are my demands. Mark them well, so that you do not forget.

"First, that you demobilize your entire Army at once.

"Second, that Naval and Air Force fleets be dispatched to the French coast, manned only by skeleton crews.

"Third, that you arrange for the receiving of regional commissioners that I shall send you to take over control of your industrial and government centers.

"Fourth, that you prepare and establish quarters for the immediate arrival of the Fourth Black Army of Control.

"And fifth, that your countrymen, including women and children, be informed that any resistance to the fulfillment of

BLACK LIGHTNING!

these demands will result in the instant death of the entire population of the state, city and community in which such resistance takes place."

The voice paused, and the weirdly uniformed figure shifted its position on the chair.

"Those are my demands. Take them at once to your President and his committee. I give you exactly five hours. You may communicate agreement to me over International Commerce wave-length number fourteen. Refuse these demands, or delay your reply beyond the five-hour limit, and my armies will hammer you all into the soil of your native land. That is all. Remember, you have five hours in which to obey!"

The masked head bobbed violently, and a black gloved fist crashed against the dial panel. Those watching saw sparks slither out in all directions.

Instantly, the picture faded, and a spinning jumble of blurred shadows smudged the screen. And then even the shadows faded into oblivion, leaving nothing but a framed blank space on the metal-laminated wall.

CHAPTER 3
WAR DECLARED!

FOR A long minute the control room virtually quivered with an almost supernatural, ringing silence. Eyes dry, lips burning, Dusty had the sudden impression that he had been looking into the vortex of a seething inferno of hell. The muscles of his body felt strangely stiff and aching, and his nerves were taut as bowstrings.

It took every ounce of his will power to tear his eyes from the Telerad screen and look at General Horner. And when he succeeded, it seemed to him that he was seeing a replica of his own expression stamped on the other's features.

Eyes gleaming with a sort of terrified awe, the general was standing poised on the balls of his feet, one hand frozen halfway up in an attempt to unclip the transmitter tube from about his neck. The other hand was doubled into a hamlike fist, as though he were going to smash against the Telerad screen.

Then slowly he realized, licked his lips nervously, and fumbled with the transmitter clip. When he spoke, his voice seemed to come from the very soles of his shoes.

"Put me through to the President, at once, Gleason. I'll take it in the next office. You all remain right here. Don't leave this room, do you understand?"

He didn't wait to hear their combined "Yes, sir!" Shoulders hunched, face suddenly aged, yet somehow still hard, the general went through the door, and slammed it shut behind him.

The action seemed to relieve the electrified tension that still flooded the room. Major Jordon started pounding his right fist into the palm of his left hand, and punctuating each wallop with a curse. Lieutenant Gleason spun a couple of dials, flipped a switch, and then began pacing up and down the room.

Only Dusty remained right where he was. But it was not from choice. His whole body was quivering with half suppressed excitement. Quivering so much that he did not dare take a step, lest he trip over his own feet and go sprawling.

"Damn him, damn his rotten hide. He killed my best friend. I saw him do it. I saw him do it!"

The words spilled off Major Jordon's lips, and his face went purple with uncontrollable rage. Dusty hardly realized what he was doing, until he heard his own voice.

"Steady, sir! It's not going to help."

The other stopped short in the middle of a curse, lips parted and jaw down. He spun, glared at Dusty, then nodded, and forced a twisted smile to his lips.

"Thanks, captain. Sorry. You should be wearing these oak leaves instead of me."

Dusty felt foolish, tried to think of something appropriate to say. But before he could, the door opened and General Horner popped back inside. He went straight up to Gleason.

"President's orders, Gleason!" he barked. "Send out word over every commercial wave-length in the national system for all commercial transmitting stations to close down. Then send out orders over military wave-lengths for stations to send in a report on the status of their areas. Send the same thing to all high seas battle squadrons, and to all Air Force scouting bases. Send it in executive emergency code. Get at it! The President and his committee are on their way over here to receive all reports direct."

Gleason spun around, and his hands flew to the maze of dials and rheostat knobs. Seconds later, a soft purring sound, that was the man's voice muffled by the lip of the transmitter tube, drifted back over his shoulder. General Horner nodded with satisfaction, and turned toward Jordon.

"Well, Jordon," he said, "it seems that we're not the only ones who have been getting a surprise. An unsigned code message came in over the State Department wave-length just ten minutes ago. 'Gutan and Miguel Locks completely destroyed by double explosion at 10:05 tonight. Canal completely blocked to navigation.' That was all. The message faded out."

"Good God!" gasped Jordon. "Then—"

"Exactly!" snapped Horner as the other fumbled for words. "It splits our Atlantic and Pacific fleets—if it's true. That's what the President has ordered me to find out. The State Department's transmitter detector couldn't get the sending station—a static jam from a super-transformer somewhere. Perhaps we can check back through relay stations. And, if it is true—"

The general paused, doubled his fist and shook it violently.

"If it is true," he repeated harshly, "it means that that war devil has struck already. It means that this five hour business was just a bluff. It means that war was declared on America six hours ago, instead of five hours from now. It'll be war, no matter what the President decides!"

He whirled and rushed over to Gleason.

"Damn it, man, aren't you getting any reports yet?"

The junior officer shook his head, and pointed at a multiple teletype message recorder.

"All wave-lengths are static jammed, sir. Look, not a single one of the tapes has moved."

"But hell!" exploded the general. "You mean there is nothing open? That every damned wave-length in the country is jammed?"

"Yes, sir," came the reply. "They all fail to register. That is, all except one, sir. And—"

"Then for God's sake, use that one!" Horner cut in on him.

"The only one open, sir," came the sharp reply, "is International Commerce wave-length number fourteen!"

The junior officer's words echoed through the room. Horner's face paled, and the corners of his mouth twitched violently.

"Fourteen!" he got out in a croaking voice. "The wave-length he said to use! Then it must be true."

AT THAT moment the door swung open and a group of men stepped inside breathlessly.

At a glance, Dusty recognized them all. He'd seen them face to face, or their pictures in the nation's papers, countless times. They were the elected or Presidential-appointed heads of the government, the military, the Navy, and the Air Force Departments. And the first to enter was the President himself.

A wild thrill of pride surged through Dusty as he saw the grim, determined set of what was usually a pleasant, smiling face; the hard glint in the deep gray eyes and the man-against-man swing of the broad shoulders.

For a fleeting second he forgot about the crisis of impending doom that seemed to lurk in the very air that he breathed. He forgot it in one great moment of untarnished admiration for the executive leader of his own native land—his President.

But the President had eyes only for General Horner.

BLACK LIGHTNING!

"What have you received so far, General?"

The words snapped off the tight lips like nickel-jacketed steel bullets whipping from the muzzle of a Browning.

"Nothing, sir. All national wave-lengths are static jammed. But we're still trying."

"All? What about the wave-length he told you to—?"

"Lieutenant Gleason says its the only one open, sir."

With a wave of his hand for silence, the President stepped past Horner and went over to the control-room officer.

"Lieutenant Gleason, send this message over to Fourteen. Ready? To the commander of the Black Invaders. Sir, the Government of the United States of America refuses every one of your demands. We hereby declare that a state of war exists between this country and your forces. Signed, the President and the Congressional Committee."

Turning toward the others, the President eyed them in silence for a minute. Then his lips moved and he spoke.

"The die has been cast, gentlemen. Our country is now at war. May God in Heaven give us guidance, comfort and courage, and lead us through it all to a complete and final victory for the cause we and our countrymen forever hold closest to our hearts. Amen."

As though a hidden spring had been suddenly pressed, every man in the room stiffened to attention and saluted solemnly, as an echoing "Amen" came from the innermost regions of their hearts.

Fired with a love of country and right far greater than he

had ever dreamed he could possess, Dusty Ayres stood enthralled in the gloriousness and drama of the moment.

And then, suddenly, he was almost jerked off his feet. General Horner had him by the arm, and was practically dragging him out through the door.

"It's up to you, now, Ayres!" the general's words hissed against his eardrums, as he raced down the steel lined corridor. "We haven't got a second to lose. They're probably on their way right now. Remember, don't stop at anything. Contact the corps area commanders at all costs. You must not fail. Shoot anything or anyone that gets in your way, understand? Here, this will identify you to all."

A square card was jammed into Dusty's hand. He was only able to get a glimpse of the U.S. Government seal countersigned with the President's own signature, before Horner made him shove it in his pocket.

At the elevators, General Horner skidded to a stop, practically threw Dusty into one with its doors open, and then pivoting, grabbed the gawking sentry.

"Escort this officer to the military field!" he barked. "There's a staff car at the curb, waiting. Don't let anything stop you. Go through, and go through fast. My orders!"

The sentry hadn't completed half of his nod before Horner shoved him into the elevator and slammed the door shut. A split second later, electric mechanism clicked and the elevator shot downward. Had not Dusty unconsciously braced himself he would have gone crashing up against the guard railing.

As it was, he still didn't have his breath when the car slid to a full stop at the ground floor, and the doors flew open. But the sense of action within him was clicking over at lightning speed. He reached over and jerked the sentry after him.

"Come on, soldier!" he clipped out. "Here's where we travel!"

Feet smacking the tiled flooring, they raced through the lobby, barged through the heavy doors and tore down the long flight of stone steps to the curb.

A non-com, lounging behind the wheel of a staff car, jerked to attention and jabbed the synchro-gear mesh button.

"The military field!" Dusty barked at him, and piled into the rear seat.

The red-faced panting soldier was almost flung back onto the sidewalk as the car leaped forward. But by the grace of God and Dusty's hand shooting out to grab him, he regained his balance and tumbled inside.

By now the car was roaring through the capital's streets, its siren scattering white-faced pedestrians to the left and right.

Rubber shrieked in protest as it sliced around corners, and a hundred and one new blockades swept toward them with each passing second. But the non-com at the wheel knew his job, and obviously he had received his orders. Eyes glued to the road ahead, he gave the car all it could take.

"My gosh, sir, look! Someone's following us!"

DUSTY WHIRLED at the soldier's wild exclamation, and glanced through the rear window. The soldier was right. A jet black car of strange make was streaking after them, missing the same crash dangers with equal skill, and whipping around every corner they took.

One glance and Dusty knew beyond a doubt that the pursuing car was not government. Just why he knew that, he didn't bother to explain to himself. He just knew it—knew that the hidden occupants of that car were after him. Like a flash of light the general's warning came back to him. "Once you leave here, you travel with death!"

His heart leaped up to the back of his throat to choke him, and the palms of his hands went wet and clammy. Unseen eyes had been watching his every move since he left his home drome. With a start, he remembered that he had not even spoken to General Horner about the sky attacker. Perhaps if he had spoken—

But hell, what did it matter now? In the last sixty seconds the low black car had gained sixty yards. Black? Good God, was that a symbol of the Black Invaders?

With a curse, Dusty leaned toward the driver.

"We're being followed!" he yelled above the whine of the powerful engine under the hood. "Give it everything you've got. We've got to lose them!"

An almost imperceptible jerk of the non-com's head indicated that he had heard. A split second later Dusty went slamming up against the side of the back seat, as the car split-arced around the next corner. Before he could pick himself up, he went flying over on top of the soldier as the car raced around a second and opposite corner. Then like a streak of light it went whamming down a straight-away stretch.

"Atta boy, Corporal!" the soldier shouted. "You gained some on them, then."

Dusty looked back, and tingled with momentary relief. The black car had lost twice what it had gained at the start. But at that instant a stream of jetting flame spewed out from behind its windshield. Dusty grabbed the sentry and pulled him down onto the floor. A split second later the glass in the rear window became a mass of criss-cross cracks.

"Thanks, sir!" panted the sentry as he scrambled up. "But this car is armored. They can't do nothing unless they get abreast of us, or in front. So long as we keep in the lead, it's okay. And—"

But Dusty wasn't listening. Through the cracked glass he saw the black car turn off the main highway and go tearing up a tangent street. In another moment he lost it from view. He slid back onto the seat, and heaved a sigh.

"They turned off, Corporal!" he yelled. "Good work!"

"No, it ain't yet, sir," the astonishing reply whipped back to him. "That street swings in about a mile ahead. It's up to us to beat them to the corner. We'll do it, sir. You just hang on."

The icy fingers of a new dread circling his heart, Dusty sat rigid, swaying with the car as though he were actually a fixed part of it. Beside him, the sentry was a crouched image of stone.

It seemed an eternity, though it was only a matter of seconds, before his straining eyes saw the converging point of the two highways up ahead. And even as he saw it, a wild cry rang from his lips. A milk lorry blocked their side of the road, and off to his left, thundering down to the converging point on the other side of the road, was the black car.

Faintly he heard the non-com driver's cry of warning.

"Get hold of something back there! We're going right through!"

A ribbon of road whipping toward him—the massive hulk of a milk lorry—a black streak whipping in at a tangent. Those three things flashed across Dusty's brain as he automatically braced himself.

And then it happened.

The milk lorry shot past their right side. There was a high-keyed whine of ripping metal. A fraction of a second later the black shadow careened into their left side, slid off and seemed to disappear through the front of a building. Then there was a loud crack. A human voice screamed with mortal pain, and the non-com driver fell over like a poled ox.

Instinctive action shot Dusty forward. His frantic fingers found the wheel, gripped it, only to be wrenched off as the wheel bucked, and the car lurched sidewise.

He had the crazy sensation that a thousand steel hooks were looped in his body, each one pulling in a different direction. Something smashed against the top of his skull, and set his brain on fire. Choking, sobbing, cursing, he slumped downward.

CHAPTER 4
MYSTERY ORDERS

"HEY, MIKE, this one's breathing!"

The words rolled into Dusty's fogged senses from a long way off. In a dulled sort of way his brain registered the fact that hands had taken hold of him; that he was being lifted clear of a bed of spear points and carried through soft, limitless space.

"One of them Air Force fellows, eh? Well, no wonder. They're a crazy lot for speed."

The words seemed to touch a secret spring in Dusty's head. He suddenly realized that his eyes were open; that he was looking at a pair of weather-beaten faces. Each face was topped off by a shiny black-visored blue cap, with a silver badge in front. He scowled at the inscription on the silver badges, then grunted as the meaning came home to him. Each inscription read—Motor Police Patrol, District of Columbia.

"Now take it easy, Captain," said one of the weather-beaten faces. "It's mighty lucky you're alive. What's the idea of going so fast, anyway?"

The last question unloosened a flood of memory in Dusty's brain. He gasped, and pushed away the hands that tried to hold him.

"That black car!" he exclaimed. "They're secret agents. I've got to get to the military field."

"Secret agents, eh?" growled one of the policemen. "Well, they ain't doing anything secret now. All three of them is dead. And so are the two lads that were with you, Captain."

Bushy brows furrowed, and a pair of skeptical eyes peered into Dusty's.

"Huh! Suppose you come along and tell the desk lieutenant all about it!"

Dusty's head was ringing like a four alarm fire. He had to

go to the military field. But what for? That's what he couldn't remember.

"I've got to get to the military field!" he blurted out wildly. "I've got to get there."

"Well," dubiously from one of the motor policemen, "you won't be riding in either of these wrecks. Suppose you come along with us, Captain, and get that cut on your forehead fixed up. You're in no shape to go any place for a while."

Dusty groaned helplessly. The staff car was twisted about a fire hydrant, its long, streamlined hood less than three feet from a building front. Twenty yards down the street, the rear end of the jet black car poked out from a great hole in a store front. There was a crowd collecting about it, and staring with eerie fascination as a squad of grim-faced policemen took three limp and twisted bodies from the wreckage. A city ambulance was at the curb, and on the sidewalk near it, two blanket-covered stretchers. Beneath each blanket was a huddled form.

But one thing that caught Dusty's roving eyes was an Army rifle lying in the gutter close to the staff car. He gazed at it, striving desperately to reason out why the sight of it stirred an elusive thought in his brain.

And then, like a bolt of lightning striking home, he recalled everything. With a choked cry he glanced at his wrist watch. The hands under the non-shatterable glass showed exactly seven twenty-five. Good God, he'd left the War Department at six-thirty! Almost an hour lost already!

With one hand he grabbed a motor patrolman's arm. The

other he shoved into his pocket, pulled out the card Horner had given him, and waved it in front of the man's face.

"The military field, quick!" he snapped. "We're going in your patrol car!"

The other glanced at the card, and his eyes popped with utter astonishment.

"Sure, sir, sure!" he gasped out. "I can get you there in five minutes. Gee, sir, why didn't you show me that before?"

Dusty didn't bother to answer. Dragging the policeman after him, he ran over to the parked patrol car, and slid in behind the wheel. The policeman hesitated a split second, then leaped on the running board, braced himself with one hand, and grabbed the siren handle with the other.

The motor patrolman had said five minutes, but it was only three minutes later when Dusty tore across the composition tarmac of the military field, and rubber-screamed to a full stop at the side of his plane.

A field mechanic ran over, helped him out, and gaped.

"Gosh, skipper, something happen? We got orders to tune her up about an hour ago!"

"Plenty!" snapped Dusty over his shoulder, as he legged into his ship. "Tell the field dispatcher that I haven't got time to wait for his 'All Clear.' If he raises hell with you, refer him to General Horner."

Kicking the wheel lock release, Dusty heeled the throttle and air compensator forward in one swift motion. The twenty-five hundred horses cowled into the nose took it without a single kickback, and the Silver Flash leaped forward, seemed to virtually set itself, and then went tearing up into a cloud-fleck-ed dawn sky.

WITH ALMOST a whole hour of precious time already wasted, he didn't bother about altitude. At ten thousand he checked the climb, leveled off and set his directional compass indicator for a straight line route to Atlanta, Georgia. That done with, he started to turn his short wave radio finder knob.

To his ears came nothing but a high-keyed buzz. His heart pounded against his ribs, then seemed to sink within him. The air over America was still being jammed by some hidden high-powered transformer set.

One after the other he tried to tune in on the military station settings, but to all he got the same telltale buzz.

Leaving the switch open, so that he'd be sure to pick up anything from a station that might succeed in breaking through the static wave wall, he leaned back against the headrest and stared fixedly at the Virginia and North Carolina terrain sweep-ing toward him from out of the distance.

Atlanta would be his first stop. Perhaps he'd get news there. They had a powerful station in that area, and perhaps they'd received a relay message from the government station in the Canal Zone. If the canal was blocked, there would be hell to pay.

He jerked up straight, as a new thought came to him. Why, damn it, what could be a better place for an attack than right in the Canal Zone? It would be a perfect base of operations for the Black Invaders. From there they could work north through Mexico, and smash into the American Southwest. And with their sea fleets working up and down the Atlantic and the Pacific coasts, the whole country could be bottled up and blockaded. Why, hell, sure—

"Wait a minute, fellow!" his own voice rapped at him aloud. "You just stick to your job, and let Washington H.Q. figure out all the tricky angles!"

But when at last he tore earthward toward the Atlanta field he had figured out no less than a hundred different ways for Fire-Eyes to completely cripple the United States, and do it almost overnight.

The instant he touched ground and wheel-braked to a stop, a car rushed out to him. A thin man in general's uniform practically leaped clear of the front seat and ran up to him. Dusty recognized him at once as Brigadier Allen, the corps area commander.

"Well, Captain Ayres?"

Black eyes probed into his own.

"Seven, sir," said Dusty in low tones. "Anything from the Canal Zone, sir?" he blurted out a second later. "Washington H.Q. is static jammed."

The other scowled at him.

"What?" he snapped. "Canal Zone? What about it?"

Dusty started to speak, then checked himself.

"Nothing, sir," he said. "Stand clear. Taking off!"

The general bellowed a question after him, but Dusty didn't hear it. He was already clearing ground and swinging southwest toward the New Orleans corps area.

There he delivered his secret number, asked the same question, and got the same astonished question in reply. And it was even the same at the El Paso area. At Los Angeles, too, where the most powerful military station of all was established. No one knew anything.

Racing up the Southern California coast toward the San Francisco area, he battled silently with the countless tricky questions that spun and whirled about in his head.

The four important southern areas had been contacted, and he had learned absolutely nothing. Not that it was his duty to find out. Yet a strange sense of dread gripped him as though it were the jaws of a steel vise relentlessly closing in.

Somewhere, the fist of disaster was hovering, waiting the right moment to smash down. He knew it! Damn it, he could feel it. It was all about him. In the air that tore past his wings. Burning deep in the eyes of those he met during his brief stops on the ground. A steel fist hovering. Where? Had it really smashed down on the Panama Canal? Had it—?

God, that was the thing, the very thing that seemed to consume his brain with white fire. He didn't know. No one else knew. Communication was cut off—the air jammed. A whole country waiting—waiting—waiting for what? Waiting for news. That was it.

Suddenly the tangled mess of thought fled from his brain, and a great charge of high-tension excitement streaked through him. The perpetual buzzing had ceased in his earphones. Different sounds were coming through—the sounds of a human voice. It was too fuzzy for him to get at first.

Steeling his trembling fingers, he bent over the oscillation knob on the wave-length panel and moved it a hair to the right. The sounds started to fade out. He moved it a hair to the left of the true setting, and dampened the magnetic shield adjustment. And then, a split second later, clear reception came to him. Every nerve tensed, he listened as a distant voice came to him through the earphones.

"… forty-two degrees west. Position due south of Jamaica. Four squadrons of heavy armored battle cruisers, with advance escort of twelve airplane carriers. It is believed that this enemy force is proceeding for attack on Colon. Canal already destroyed. Second 10th, 12th, 16th, and 20th Atlantic squadrons will proceed to this point at once. New Orleans air groups 6, 8, and 11 are proceeding to Canal Zone now. Enemy is reported to be—"

DUSTY GROANED as the words faded out. He fumbled and fooled with the dial setting, but it was almost a minute before they came back. But it was not the same voice. His set was on a different wave setting.

As he glanced at the dial his heart leaped over with frenzied excitement. He was getting emergency orders to base air units direct from Air Force H.Q. in Washington. The blood raced and whirled through his veins as the words came in.

"Altitude bombers, Groups 10, 14, and 15 will proceed for concentration at Frisco. High speed attack units will concentrate at Los Angeles. These will include all units in West Coast zone. Gas bombers, Groups 4, 5, and 6 will concentrate at Tacoma. Transport units will serve all three areas, and contact mobile transport battalions 24, 30, and 40. Proceed immediately. End of message. 7A 64, Washington."

The earphones clicked and went silent. Dusty gaped at the wave-length panel. His brows furrowed.

"But what the hell?" he blurted out aloud. "What about my gang, H.S. Group 7? You can't do without them. They deserve first crack. They're the best outfit in the whole damned Air Force!"

The burst of protest off his chest, he leaned back and shook his head sadly. What the hell was he yelling about? A damned good thing he didn't have the two-way switch up, or maybe somebody would have heard him sounding off on his own ideas.

But hell, his gang should be in on it. If the attack was coming from the West Coast, they should be.

A cry of amazement slid off his lips, and he jerked up straight in the seat. West Coast? Good God, he was on the West Coast right now!

He stared out at the broad expanse of the Pacific down off to his left. Close in to shore he could see three squadrons of American Navy ships, riding peacefully at formation anchorage.

Five miles out were the dim shapes of an airplane carrier unit, strung out in a line that lost both of its ends in a heavy sea mist. And beyond them—nothing but the limitless swells of the Pacific.

Yes, he was right smack over the West Coast. But it was a picture he'd seen a million times at least. The ships out there were riding at anchor as though a Presidential review were expected—too damned close in to shore for adequate defense maneuvering.

Yet he'd heard with his own ears the Washington Air H.Q. order for concentration on the West Coast. It didn't take a military expert to figure out the idea behind it. It meant in plain English that Washington expected an attack on the West Coast, and they were ordering adequate defense to that area.

Quivering with a new excitement, Dusty shot his Silver Flash toward the San Francisco corps area landing field. Perhaps Intelligence had remade contact with Agent 10. And, perhaps, down there on the Frisco field, orders were waiting for him to terminate his special mission, and hold himself ready for active duty in that area—the area that would receive the first blow of war.

However, even as the thrill of excited expectation danced through his body, he realized in his heart that such a possibility just couldn't come true. No matter what might be happening elsewhere, his job was to keep on going. His orders were to go through; not to stop at anything!

Hell, he wished that his group major had picked one of the other boys for this messenger job. He wanted to be sent where there was action, not go slamming around the country saying, "Seven, sir" to a lot of pop-eyed corps area commanders.

Action, that's what he wanted. His fingers itched to press the electric firing switch of his guns. To hear their chattering yammer, and to see some enemy ship quiver and tremble as the rain of death from his guns slashed into it.

Yet, even as he told himself those things, the soldier in him refused to believe. No, the thing he wanted to do most was to serve his country in the very best way he could. Why, what was he thinking of, anyway? Hadn't he been given a great honor? The honor of being the first airman to be assigned active duty in time of war?

Hadn't he heard the President's message to Fire-Eyes, with his own ears? And did he think that this menace that was encircling America would be brushed away in one effort? Hell no! Every red-blooded American would see plenty of action before this thing was over.

Rapping the stick, he sent the Silver Flash side-slipping downward.

"Yeah!" he growled. "You stick to your knitting, Dusty, and like it, see?"

FIVE SECONDS later he braked to a quick stop in the middle of the field. Sliding open the glass hood, he lifted himself out of the cockpit, by way of stretching his cramped legs, and waited for the staff car that was speeding across the field.

As it drew near he recognized the commander, Brigadier Fulton. But it was the third figure in the car that brought an exclamation of joy to his lips. For the man was none other than Colonel "Hammer-Head" Harmsworth, a former group commander, and, as a matter of fact, the man who had taught him to fly. He hadn't seen him for over two years.

As the car coasted to a stop, the two officers jumped out and sprinted the rest of the way. Dusty grinned at his old instructor and snapped his hand up in salute. At about the same instant, Brigadier Fulton's voice cracked out at him:

"Damn the formalities, Captain Ayres! What is it?"

Dusty reddened. He hadn't even looked at the Brigadier.

"Sorry, sir!" he choked. "It's seven."

With a quick nod the other spun around, almost bowled over Colonel Harmsworth, and dashed back to the car. The colonel made no effort to follow. Instead he came close to the cockpit, smiled, and nodded in admiration.

"Congratulations, Dusty," he said. "I'm glad that one of my old pupils was selected for the first air job. But I envy you, too. It's a hell of a note for Washington to ground us all until further orders. Say, where'd you get that cut on your head?"

"Motor mix-up," said Dusty hurriedly. "But did you say that you were all grounded?"

"Yes," replied Harmsworth. "Orders came through an hour ago, by ground wire, along with news about the declaration of war by the President. Every unit on the West Coast has been grounded. I've just been raising hell. We should all be on patrol— Ayres, get out of that ship! You're hurt, man!"

Dusty shook his head.

"No, no, Colonel," he insisted, "I'm all right. You mean that you've just been talking with Washington Air Force H.Q. and they grounded all units?"

"Right!" the other nodded. "Until further orders. I'd say that you're the only pilot in the whole Air Force who is flying right now."

Dusty grabbed the colonel's arm.

"Something's wrong, sir! I just heard Washington order half

of the central area air units to proceed here to the West Coast
for concentration! What about that?"

The other's eyes blazed.

"You heard what?" he roared. "Why, you're crazy, man!"

"I'm not crazy!" Dusty cut in. "Look, there on the panel, I
left it at the Washington wave-length reading. Three altitude
bomber groups, all highspeed attack units, three gas bomber
groups, and transport units for ground contact work. I heard
the orders, Colonel, and the sign-off signal 7A64, Washington!"

Harmsworth's face paled, went beet-red, then paled again as
he peered fiercely at Dusty. His lips moved but he didn't say
anything. Then presently the words came, low and husky.

"If you're in your right mind, Ayres, then something is wrong.
Washington Air Force H.Q. couldn't possibly have sent out
those orders!"

"No," he repeated a moment later, "they couldn't possibly
have done it! Why, damn it, I switched off ground wire connection with them as you were coming in to land. And they
had just told me that further orders would come by ground, as
the air east was static-jammed. By God, Dusty, I think you've
stumbled into an enemy attempt to leave the East wide open
for their first attack!"

"You mean, Colonel—?"

"I mean," the other cut in before the question was finished,
"that it's a sure thing that the Black Invaders did this. Why,
hell, their logical attack would come on the East, anyway. They'd
be starting out from Europe."

"But, I don't understand, Colonel. Why the devil wasn't what I got picked up at this station?"

Harmsworth scowled.

"God knows. Unless—"

"Unless what, sir?"

"Unless this static jam just covers the ground, doesn't extend upward. As far as I know, your ship is the only one that's been up. If you were above the static blanket you'd get reception, while on the ground here, we couldn't."

"I got more than one message, sir!" Dusty exclaimed, as he suddenly remembered. "I think the other was from the Navy Department. It was a general order to the Atlantic battle squadrons to proceed toward the Canal. It said that Black Invader forces were concentrating south of Jamaica, for a probable attack on the Canal. Then it faded out on me."

For a moment the other made no comment. Eyes narrowed speculatively, he remained deep in thought.

"An attack on the Canal, eh?" he murmured presently. "And if that, too, is a fake, it would mean that our Atlantic squadrons would be pulled away from the East Coast. Listen, Dusty, what are your next stops?"

"Tacoma, Bismarck, Chicago, Boston, and New York, sir," the pilot answered promptly.

Harmsworth stepped down off the wing.

"I'm going to check back on this thing," he said. "Washington H.Q. is either asleep, or else they're walking into a wide-open trap. I'll contact you at Bismarck, if anything turns up. Let her rip, son, and good luck."

With a smile and a nod, the colonel turned and ran across the field. Dusty hesitated a second, then opened up the throttle. Like something actually human and impatient to be away, the Silver Flash streaked across the ground and raced upward.

CHAPTER 5
X34

A LITTLE over an hour later he slid down onto the landing strip at Tacoma, Washington. All the time the two-way switch of his panel had been open, but nothing had come to him out of the air. It was as though the world of radio communication had gone completely dead. A queer sense of relief and comfort stole over him as he watched the corps area commander's car speed out onto the field.

"Are you Captain Ayres?"

The bemedaled figure that leaped out of the car and ran up fairly shouted the question.

Dusty nodded and started to speak, but the other cut him off.

"Let me see your identification!"

Frowning, Dusty pulled the card from his pocket and held it up. The other, whom Dusty now placed as General Baker, peered at it intently, then nodded and gave a grin of satisfaction.

"Right, Captain," he said. "Here, this came by ground wire half an hour ago."

The man held out a folded slip of yellow paper. Dusty took it, smoothed it out.

BLACK LIGHTNING!

To Captain Ayres
c/o Corps Area Commander,
Tacoma Area.

Your orders reversed. Report to me at once.

Signed, X34.

Dusty read it twice, glanced questioningly at the general.

"You say this came by ground wire, sir?" he asked.

"It did," was the short reply. "Half an hour ago."

"But I don't understand, sir! My orders were to go through, regardless."

"No use now," replied the other. "Washington knows the point of attack. It's the Canal Zone. Our Atlantic fleet is now on its way to cut them off. Lucky devils, the Navy! We're to stay mobilized as we are until further orders."

In a few right-to-the-point sentences, Dusty recounted his experience south of Frisco and his conversation with Colonel Harmsworth. As he talked, the look of annoyed patience that had stamped the general's face from the beginning faded and changed to one of genuine alarm. He motioned Dusty out of the plane.

"Come with me, Captain," he said. "I think it's best that we check back on this before you do anything."

Cutting his engine, Dusty legged out and followed the general over to the car. In silence they rode to Corps H.Q., got out, and hurried into the signal room. An operator working over a radio switch board turned as they entered.

"Can't even get Frisco, sir," he said to the general. "But the blanketing seems to be local. Every now and then I pick up a code signal from the St. Louis station. But it fades out on me before I can get anything."

"Well, never mind that!" snapped the general. "Get War Department, Washington, on the ground wire. Emergency signal."

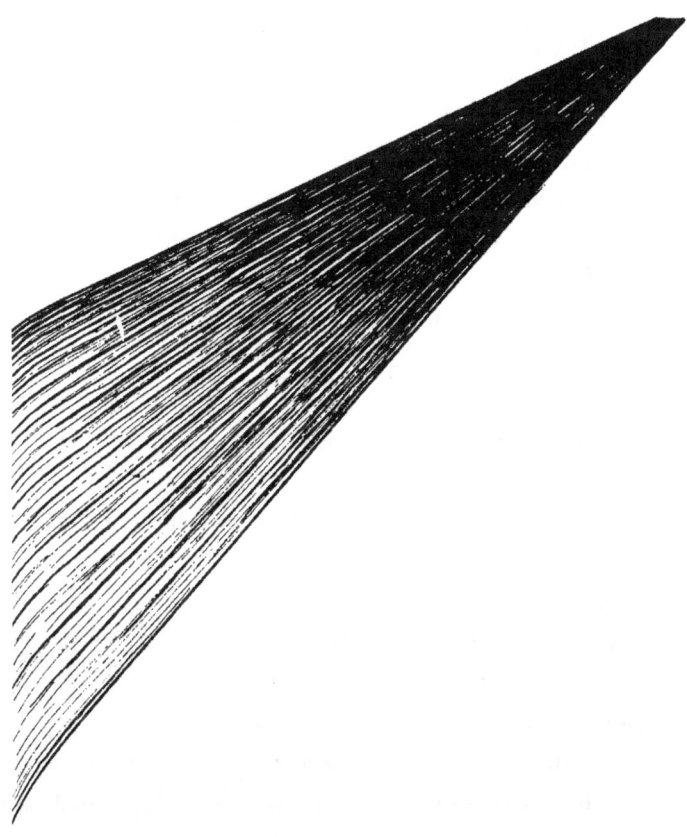

"Yes, sir," nodded the operator, and went over to his old-fashioned telegraph keyboard.

A minute later the spark gap crackled with dots and dashes going out on the line. The operator repeated four times, then switched over to the receiving key. Face expectant, he waited for the acknowledge of his call signal to click through. But there came nothing but silence. The tapper-knob on the instrument didn't so much as even quiver.

The operator muttered something, swung the switch to sending, and repeated his signal. Again he stopped, again he listened and waited expectantly, and again, nothing but silence.

The silence was eventually broken by a harsh snort from General Baker.

"What the devil's the matter? Can't you get them?"

The operator shrugged and shook his head.

"It's mighty funny sir," he frowned. "The line seems to be dead. As a matter of fact, I'm not so sure that my own signals are going out."

"Then for God's sake, make sure!" snapped the general. "Try a relay through Frisco or Bismarck—or any other damned station. But, get through somehow!"

"Yes, sir," he answered meekly.

Five minutes later the operator jerked out the connection plug, and allowed it to hang uselessly by its cord.

"Sorry, sir," he said, "I can't raise a single station. There's a break in the transcontinental line somewhere. My signals are just going to a dead end."

The senior officer growled something, grabbed up the radio phone at his elbow and banged down the plug-in switch. Instantly an eerie screeching sound started to pour out of the transmitter.

General Baker gave a yelp and leaped backward, his face white. The operator jumped over and knocked up the plug-in switch. The sound died out at once.

"Good God!" gasped the shaking general. "What in the devil did that?"

The operator didn't answer for a moment.

"That sound, sir," he whispered finally, "was caused by someone opening a transformer all the way. It was nothing but a drown-out signal. Only twice as bad as we've been getting on the teletype machine."

"But where is that transformer?" demanded the other. "We've got to hunt it out—arrest whoever's operating it. Damn it, we're practically isolated here!"

"That's just what we are, sir," nodded the operator slowly. "Isolated. And where that transformer station is, sir, I haven't any idea. It could be five miles from here, or five hundred. All they have to do, you see, sir, is tune in on our wave-length, and keep their power on. But there's one thing, as long as they jam our wave-length they can't get through to anyone themselves."

The general bit off an irate curse.

"Damn lot of good that does us!" he rapped out.

"I wonder if we're the only ones, sir," Dusty put in suddenly.

The other spun on him.

"What do you mean?"

"I mean, sir," began Dusty slowly, "have the Blacks tried to isolate every one of the corps areas? With the exception of Frisco, no place where I've landed had any official news. With every place isolated, this flight of mine would be a dead loss, because mobilization contact afterward would be impossible."

He paused a second and tapped the dispatch he still held in his hand.

"Maybe that's the reason for this, sir," he said. "Perhaps Washington has found that out—and is calling me back. Frankly, I don't know what to think. It's all so jumbled up."

"Well, anyway," nodded the other vigorously, "you've got your orders."

Dusty stared helplessly at the teletype dispatch.

"I wonder," he muttered, "if I have."

"Of course you have!" barked the other. "It's signed by X34, isn't it?"

"Yes, sir," nodded Dusty. "But I wonder if X34 sent it, General. It kind of strikes me funny that just half an hour ago messages came into this station perfectly, and now when we want to check back we find all communication at a standstill. Did X34 really send this? I'm going to try and find out. If I can't, then I'm going to obey my original orders."

The other shrugged his shoulders.

"Suit yourself, Captain. I wash my hands of it. Your orders come from Washington, the same as mine, so my units will stick here until we confirm those orders."

Dusty saluted and walked out.

THREE MINUTES later he was in his ship. He took a last look over at the H.Q. buildings, and saw General Baker running around, barking a string of orders. He grunted with disgust.

"The old Army pass-the-buck game, eh? With all your initiative, Baker, you're going to be a big help in this war!"

With a nod for emphasis he heeled the throttle open and sent the Silver Flash skimming forward. Once clear of the ground he set the automatic climb control and gave all of his attention to his wave-length panel.

From the ground all the way up to thirty thousand feet he got nothing but jammed air. But at thirty-five thousand the earphones crackled to life. Then suddenly, as he made a finer adjustment of the wave-length setting, he received the rapid-fire dot-dashing of a code wireless station.

He tried desperately to pick out some of the letters and make words out of them, but it was impossible. After five minutes of steady concentration he knew definitely that the sender was not using the International code.

As that thought came to him, he suddenly stiffened in the seat. He remembered reading somewhere in an article, about a secret, wireless dot-dash code the Black Invaders were using in Europe. It was reported to be considerably simpler than standard International Morse, and could therefore be sent out faster.

But hell, he couldn't be picking up any stuff the Blacks were sending out. His receiver only had a range of about four thousand miles, and the Black Invaders were in Europe.

Wide-eyed, he stared at the station directional finder needle, and twirled the power indicator. The result seemed to mock his fogged brain. According to the needle reading, he was listening in to a station located about two thousand miles east of his present position. In other words, somewhere between Detroit and New York.

"But that can't be!" he mouthed into his oxygen tube. "I must be imagining things."

But he wasn't, and he knew he wasn't. Somewhere between

Detroit and New York, an enemy station was sending out high-altitude signals. Undoubtedly it was a secret station operated by the Black agents General Horner had spoken about.

But the one fact that sent an icy chill rippling down Dusty's spine was that he'd only been able to pick up the signals on a thirty-five thousand foot wave-length adjustment. That meant that the ground station must be in communication with aircraft at that altitude!

Stunned for the moment, Dusty could only turn his head and gaze out at the vast limitless space through which he was racing. He saw nothing but thin air, and the cloud layer drifting by far below him. Yet he suddenly became possessed with a queer sensation—a feeling that at any second he would see a squadron of battle planes come tearing into view. He grunted a curse and tried to rid himself of the dizzy premonition.

"Cut it, Dusty!" he grated aloud. "What the hell's the matter, letting every damned little thing get you? A swell soldier you're turning out to be!"

Rapping on the stick, he sent the Silver Flash streaking down to twenty thousand. There he twirled the wave-length adjuster for his own transmitter, and switched on the battery current. Then he bent close to the mouthpiece.

"Captain Ayres calling X34… Captain Ayres calling X34!"

Over and over again he repeated the call signal, and kept his eyes glued to the red signal bulb on the panel. Two minutes, three minutes dragged past, but the light did not go on. Still sending the call signal, he started flying in a slow circle.

Then, suddenly remembering what the Tacoma operator had

said, he turned the dial reading to the signal for the St. Louis Army station. And still he got no reply.

One by one he went down the whole list of receiving stations, but the red light didn't wink once. Nor did a change of altitude help any. He even went up to forty thousand, stood the cold air and dizziness as long as he could, and then slid down again with no results.

A glance at the magnetic watch on the dash told him that it was about 12:45 p.m. Almost six hours of flying time gone, and here he was chasing around in circles over northern Wyoming, striving desperately to make contact with some ground station.

The X34 dispatch in his pocket seemed to virtually burn a hole in his side. In the next five minutes he pulled it out and read it at least fifty times. And the message was always the same—"Your orders reversed. Report to me at once!"

DAMMIT, HE had to know first. Too many things were happening for him to just take a chance on his own judgment. He couldn't possibly make Washington under four hours, going full out. And then if he should find that he was wrong, that the message was a fake, the wrath of General Horner, and a lot of other unpleasant things would come down on his head! The general had told him to trust no one; that he was to go through at any cost, that any other orders didn't matter. He, Dusty, was to contact the ten corps area commanders.

Yet, countermanding orders had arrived at Tacoma before he had. And General Baker hadn't even asked him for the secret number. Didn't that mean—

He left the thought unfinished as the red signal light on the panel suddenly winked. Feverishly he bent over the transmitter tube.

"Captain Ayres, speaking. What station's calling?"

The earphones hummed for a second or two, and then words came.

"Des Moines Air Base 23 with relay from Washington Air H.Q., 7, A, 6, 4. Are you ready, Captain Ayres?"

Dusty shot a look at the wave-length reading, and gasped. It was about thirty points off the usual reading for the Des Moines Air Base. For a second he hesitated. Then impulsively he nodded.

"Ready, Des Moines!"

"Relay from Washington," said the earphones. "You will proceed at once to Winnipeg for high-speed group concentration with Canadian forces. Message signed, X34."

"Winnipeg?" Dusty blurted into the transmitter tube. "What—that—I mean, is that all of the message?"

"Right!" came the reply. "That's all! Signing off."

"Hey wait, Des Moines!" the pilot yelled. "Wait!

But the red light went out and left him yelling into a dead wave-length. Furiously he spun the dial to the usual Des Moines reading, and called the station's signal until he was hoarse. But not once did he get a reply, not even a fade-out signal.

With a groan he leaned back wearily and tried to figure out this last and craziest order. Winnipeg? Why in the name of Heaven have a high-speed group concentration there? Des Moines must have been trying to contact some other pilot, and gotten on his wave-length by mistake. But they'd called him by name. The message had been meant for him, all right. If he could only get through to Washington direct, and check on all these orders.

He suddenly felt very tired and depressed. His head ached, and the blood-caked gash on his left temple smarted and throbbed. He should have taken time out at one of the corps areas to get it fixed up. Should have grabbed something to eat, too.

With a curse he tried to forget what he should have done. They were trivial things, now. What mattered was this new countermanding order from General Horner. What to do? Should he go on with his original job? Should he hightail for Washington? Or should he go to Winnipeg, as Des Moines had ordered him?

The more he ran the three ideas over in his mind, the more confused they became. For the second time he fervently wished that someone else had been selected for the courier job.

Then, with a gesture of savage decision, he whipped the Silver Flash around and set a dead-on course for Winnipeg. To contact that Canadian city would only take him an extra half-hour anyway. And he just had to find out where he stood. If there was no concentration there, it would mean that the Des Moines message was a fake, that some hidden enemy had been tailing him around the country. And—but what hidden enemy? Who knew he was in the air?

The question mocked him as he thought of it.

"Orders be damned!" he grated harshly. "I'm going to find out a thing or two first!"

CHAPTER 6
THE BLACK HAWK

I T HAPPENED as Dusty tore down from higher altitude, just over the Canadian line. The cloud layer was still below him, and he couldn't yet see the ground. Easing back to half throttle, he started to coast toward the cloud layer, when suddenly the red signal light on the panel winked rapidly. Seconds later a harsh voice vibrated in the earphones.

"Level off, Captain Ayres, and fly due north!"

Rigid in the seat, Dusty stared at the panel. The voice sounded like the one he had heard while enroute from the Dayton field to Washington.

"Level off, and go due north, Captain Ayres. You can't get away this time. If you think so, then look up!"

Hardly realizing what he was doing, Dusty jerked back his head and stared heavenward. As he did, a wild cry burst from his throat. Unconsciously he brushed his hand across his eyes, and stared anew. But the scene did not change!

Less than two thousand feet above him were six jet-black fighting monoplanes. They were pursuit planes, but of what make, he could not tell. He'd never seen anything like them before. Save for their single wing, faired into the center of the fuselage, they had the same beautiful streamline design of his own Silver Flash. Even in his utter bewilderment he could not

BLACK HAWK

help but admire them. Like six graceful, death-dealing hawks. They sat poised above him.

Then to his spinning brain came the harsh voice again.

"Look below you, too, Captain Ayres."

He obeyed and got the second jolt in as many minutes.

The top of the cloud layer was speckled with at least a dozen of the speedy little black monoplanes. Neither they nor the ones above had a single marking on their wings or fuselage. But they didn't need any insignia. Though he tried to convince himself that it just couldn't be possible—Dusty knew that he was looking at a pursuit unit of the Black Invaders.

For an instant stark terror gripped him. Not a muscle of his body moved, not a single thought of action came to his brain. From head to foot he suddenly became completely paralyzed. The earphones hummed and in a dull sort of way his befuddled brain registered the words.

"You see, Captain Ayres, you have a choice. It is not our wish to kill you. On the contrary, we want to take our first air prisoner alive. That is really why I did not shoot to kill last night, nor even try to chase you. We knew that there would be another chance. So, fly north as ordered, Captain. It is the safest thing for you to do."

Harsh and grating, yet without a single trace of accent, the voice beat against Dusty's eardrums. Hardly realizing it, he bent toward the transmitter tube.

"Who the devil are you?" he shouted.

The answer came back almost instantly.

"I am known by many as the Black Hawk, Captain Ayres. Perhaps you've heard of me?"

The Black Hawk! Had he ever heard of him? Dusty had an almost irrepressible desire to laugh. Who hadn't heard of him? During the two years of war in Europe, the American papers had carried almost as many accounts of the Black Hawk as they had of Fire-Eyes himself.

Like his commander-in-chief, the Black Hawk was more or less of a mystery. To friend and foe alike he had been known as the Man of a Thousand Lives. Time and time again his death had been reported. Countless eye witnesses had sworn they'd seen him go crashing to earth. Others had vowed they had seen him shot at the firing stake. And then, a day, a week, or a month afterward, he had suddenly returned to life again and continued with his weird and well-nigh miraculous feats in the air.

One thing about him was known quite definitely. It was confirmed by the Black Invader high command—the man was the supreme head of the Black Invaders' air forces. But what other functions he performed for that ravaging horde of world destroyers was merely speculation. Everyone had ideas, of course. But no one was able to prove them.

The Black Hawk—the scourge of the sky—was right above him, ordering him to surrender!

WITH A desperate effort, Dusty tried to collect his thoughts, to spur his brain to action. He was nailed like a rat in a trap. Worse than that. A rat usually went into a trap blind, but he'd gone into this one with his eyes wide open. The choice had been his and, like the dummy he was, he'd chosen the wrong thing. Damn, it was all so plain, now.

That dot-dashing he'd received had been a Black Invader ground station signaling to this monoplane unit. And undoubtedly, the Des Moines orders had come to him from the Black Hawk's own ship. As memory flashed back for a second he seemed to be able to join up the two voices. Yes, there was a similarity—the same inflection, even though one was a harsh voice and the other just commonplace.

Trapped! For a moment he didn't try to reason why. He didn't question why so much trouble should be taken over his capture. Other thoughts crowded his brain. And the most puzzling of the lot was how in the name of God did they come to be there? But there was no plausible answer for the question. This was just a dream. A dream? Look up—look down! What do you see?

The order his brain lashed at him was but additional confirmation of what he already knew. Yet, impulsively he obeyed; stared down at the black-speckled cloud layer, and up at the six darting arrows above him.

"Well, Captain Ayres, do you surrender peacefully, or must we force you down?"

The harsh voice in the earphones snapped him back to reality. Face grim, eyes like rock, he bent over the transmitter tube. With his free hand he reached out toward the dial knob on the wave-length panel. A wild and crazy idea had flashed to his brain.

"The Black Hawk, eh?" he said slowly. "How do I know this ain't a joke? I'm on important business, and I can't waste any time. Yeah, how do I know you're the Black Hawk?"

The moment of silence that greeted his words fired the tiny spark of hope that flickered within him. With trembling fingers he turned the dial so that his sending wave was timed into the War Department wave-length. That meant that every word he spoke would go out on that wave-length, and if Washington was not static jammed, they'd get both parts of this conversation.

To make doubly sure, he unhooked one of his earphones and held it clamped against the transmitter tube.

And then, in the other earphone, he heard the harsh reply.

"You may rest assured that this is no joke, Captain Ayres. And you may also realize that our patience is practically exhausted. I am giving you a chance for your life. Any sort of resistance is futile. Now, obey, at once!"

Dusty steeled his quivering nerves.

"But how did you plan this?" he spoke into the transmitter tube. "How did you plan to meet me, Captain Ayres, at longitude one zero one and latitude four nine? How did the Black Hawk get here at this point with his squadron? I don't understand. Do you mean that the Black Invaders have already landed?"

Clamping the loose earphone against the transmitter tube,

Dusty breathed a fervent prayer. If only Washington H.Q. would be able to pick up his position tip-off. If only they'd get it and realize that a Black Invader air fleet was already on the North American continent!

At that moment it seemed to him as though all heaven and earth stood still and waited. Head thrust back, he stared up at the six black planes, waited, and dully wondered which one held the famed Black Hawk.

And then as the harsh voice spoke again, his heart seemed to drop through limitless space. Like the clarion call of doom, the words came to him.

"You are wasting your time, Captain Ayres. I realize that you are trying to send word to your Washington headquarters. You see, Captain, my own voice is being recorded right back to me. And my wave-length detector tells me that your setting is for another station. But it's useless, Captain Ayres. Every ground station in America is blanketed out. No one is hearing a thing. And now, Captain, I'm signing off and coming down to show you where to land."

As the earphone made a clicking sound, Dusty saw one of the black ships above him come sliding down in a graceful, curving arc. With the utmost ease it took up a position a bit behind and to the left of the Silver Flash. No fear of impending doom could have stopped him from turning in his seat to stare at that ship, or could have quelled the true airman's thrill at seeing so beautiful a craft of the air.

So perfect were its fuselage lines that at first he didn't see the glassed-over cowling. As a matter of fact, the cockpit wasn't exactly glassed over. At least not in the same way as his own. His rounded up in the front to enable him to see straight ahead. But the cockpit cowling of the other ship was an integral part of the fuselage. From the nose to the base of the high-finned tail ran one straight, unbroken line.

The bottom part of the fuselage was the same, except for two protruding, faired-over humps that covered the pivoting joints of the retractable landing gear.

A real ship, for a real pilot, whether he be friend or foe.

BUT THE thrill that was Dusty's lasted for only a few fleeting seconds. As he saw the figure in the black plane point toward the north, the horrible reality of the situation swept back to him. Though the horror of it was doubly intensified now, he could not take his eyes off the man in the glass-cowled cockpit.

He was a big man with a face unlike any Dusty had ever seen before. The eyes were deep-sunken and close-set and the nose was hawkish. The mouth was big, at the moment, stretched back in a wide smile revealing large, fang-like teeth. Though Dusty couldn't see clearly, the man's skin seemed to be a copperish hue, and the hair that showed beneath a skull cap was as black as the cap itself.

Trapped! The thought crashed through Dusty's brain for the millionth time. And as it did, a part of him seemed to die, the other part to flare up to white heat.

From a long way off he heard his own voice bellowing savagely.

"Like hell you will! Like hell you will!"

Even as the words rasped from his lips he slammed the throttle and compensator wide open, thumped down on the right rudder pedal and hauled the stick all the way back to his stomach. The whipping motion of the ship, as it went over, almost flung him out of the seat.

As it was, he crashed his head up against the cowling brace. But his senses were already too numbed for him to feel pain. Holding the stick back, he flashed out his free hand and pressed the electric firing switch of his guns.

Instantly the twin muzzles, streamlined into the nose, started spewing out nickle-jacketed steel messengers of death—fifteen hundred to a gun, three thousand a minute for two guns. Thundering downward he saw a black shadow dart across his fixed sights. A split second later it seemed to stop dead in mid-air, as though it had slammed into some invisible barrier. The sleek, black wings ripped off like so much paper, and the bullet-shaped fuselage went screaming down into the cloud layer, like a berserk meteor of black fire.

"First blood for the Yanks. Come on you devils, come on and get me!"

Crazy, insane words blabbed off Dusty's lips as he yanked and spun the Silver Flash about in the sky. A second black dot whipped past his sights; then it went careening straight up, like a bird caught cold in mid-flight. But what it did after that, Dusty didn't know. He didn't bother to look and find out. He had only one thought in mind; one thought that sliced through his head like a spear of livid fire.

In the few seconds that had passed, he'd learned one thing.

Tricky as these black monoplanes looked, and flew, his own Silver Flash was tops in speed and maneuverability. Hell, if he'd only guessed that before, instead of wasting time trying to get word through to Washington. But it was too late now to curse his stupidity. The thing for him to do was fly the wings off the Silver Flash. Spin, twist, and whirl and shoot his way down through this Black Hawk brood, and make a landing on American ground.

Suddenly he sucked in his breath in a sharp gasp as the realization came to him that the other ships were not shooting at him. Rather they were trying to keep out of his own savage hail of death and form a sort of aerial network about him. But though this bewildered him, it did not stop his flame-spewing guns.

Around he cut in a dime turn, straight for a black monoplane. Its pilot flopped it over on wing and tried desperately to slide out of the way. But the deadly shower from that crazy Yank's guns caught him amidships and blasted the plane into a shower of black pieces which lost themselves in the cloud layer.

"Two!" roared Dusty, and pounded his free fist against the armored side of his ship. "Come on old girl, we can do it. Let 'em shoot, if they want to. So long as it isn't a lucky burst, we're okay. Come on you Silver Flash! Let's sh—"

The rest was lost in a choking gurgle. His lungs suddenly seemed to be on fire, and his throat was closing together, shutting off his wind. Sweat oozed out on his forehead and trickled down into his eyes. Then a wave of utter weariness swept over him. Nothing seemed worth the effort any more. His arms and legs were like bars of lead, which required every ounce of his strength to move. Sound crashed against his eardrum, he dully heard his own voice.

"Dusty. Dusty, damn you, snap out of it! Do you hear? Snap out of it!"

Swaying like a drunken man, he stared through the cowling glass. God, he couldn't see! Everything was a greenish-brown. No, not quite everything. There were lines of greenish-brown, criss-crossed and woven together in a weird pattern. They were in front of him, behind him, on both sides, above and below him. He was in the very center of a greenish-brown web that seemed suspended in the sky. And on the outside of the mesh was a mass of twisting and turning black shadows.

NOT A single one of the planes was trying to get inside of the web, to dart in on him and slam a death burst into his unprotected top cowling. Of course, the first burst wouldn't count. The semi bullet-proof glass would protect him for a few moments. But after constant hammering, even it would give way. After that, death would be his lot.

But not one of the black ships was firing at him. He dashed the smarting sweat from his eyes, steeled himself against the horrible burning in his chest, and searched the heavens on all sides. They—hell, they seemed to be shooting at each other. Streams of greenish-brown smoke were pouring out from the under part of the tail of each plane. That's what made the sky look so damned funny. Those streams of peculiar-looking smoke which poured out from each ship formed the cries-cross webbing that hung all about him. What in the name of—?

"I'VE BROUGHT YOU BACK FROM THE DEAD, ONCE, CAPTAIN. ARE YOU GOING TO FORCE ME TO AGAIN?"

Dusty tried desperately to think, to reason the thing out. But it was useless. A great weight was pressing down on his brain, and a sweet, penetrating smell filled his whole body. He had the wild sensation that he was inside a candy factory. The sweet smell gagged him, dulled his senses, and steadily sapped his strength.

At that moment his guns jammed, but he didn't try to clear them. An overpowering numbness pinned him back against the seat. And his churning brain didn't seem to care. It refused to concentrate on any one thing for more than a split second at a time. Even when it dully registered the fact that he was completely shrouded by the greenish-brown mesh, that he couldn't even see the black monoplanes any longer, the reaction was a blank.

He was going down, that was all. Slipping, sliding, hurtling earthward. That was swell. Sure, wasn't it something like that that he planned to do a while ago? The idea played hide and seek in the dim recesses of his brain. That's just what he wanted to do—get down and land, then go to sleep. God, but he was tired. Felt as though he could sleep for a thousand years. Sleep, sleep, and then more sleep.

For a moment his brain clicked over normally. Damn, there was something he was supposed to do, wasn't there? Sure, but what was it? Darned if he could remember. He was in the air, in the Silver Flash. That's funny, what was he doing—a test flight perhaps? Or had he been tuning the ship up for a new crack at the speed record? His head hurt so damned much he couldn't even think. Needed fresh air—that was it. God, if he could only get his hands up and unhook the sliding cowling. No, he couldn't—funny—what the hell was the matter?

Brain deadened completely, and instinct alone guiding his grip on the controls, Dusty went thundering into the cloud layer. Seconds later he raced into clear air. He sucked it into his lungs with the feverishness of a drowning man, and a hidden lock within him seemed to snap open. But only for an instant. And then the great overpowering sense of drowsiness engulfed him again.

With a tremendous effort he forced his head to the side of the cockpit, looked out and down. Below was the panorama of dull-colored earth. The location didn't even occur to him. He had eyes only for a strip good enough to land on. That's all he wanted—to land and go to sleep.

After that, time lost all meaning to him. Perhaps it was seconds, perhaps hours, it might even have been an eternity before the wheels of the plane touched a smooth surface and he braked to a gentle stop. A sob of relief welled up within him. Ah, now he could sleep.

Later, he'd take off again—take off and go back—go back—go—

The tiny thread of consciousness snapped and Dusty went floating outward on a great, billowing cloud of utter bliss and silence.

CHAPTER 7
THE SECRET DROME

L IQUID FIRE sliding down his throat dragged Dusty back to partial consciousness. He coughed and gagged and sputtered, but his mouth seemed to be held in a vise. More liquid fire went down his throat. He tried to pry his eyes open, but the lids seemed glued together. Wildly he thrashed outward with his hands, struck something soft and yielding. And then his hands, too, were clamped down at his sides.

There was a great roaring in his ears, and his whole body seemed ready to burst apart from the pressure of the seething flames which were consuming him inside.

Then suddenly, the burning sensation left him and his whole body became as a solid form of ice. Seconds later, a strange tingling freshness swept over him, a curtain of darkness was lifted from his brain and eyes, and he found himself staring wide-eyed down the long room.

It was a queer room. The walls contained row after row of black cabinets, some of them with their doors open. The ceiling was arched and spotted with huge indirect lighting globes. Below the arched ceiling was a criss-cross net of fine copper wire, stretched straight across from wall to wall, and drawn so taut, that it gave the appearance of a solid sheet of copper. Only the lights above it belied that impression.

But what held Dusty's attention more were the figures seated in front of each wall cabinet. They were all dressed the same, in loose-fitting black uniforms and black skull caps. And fastened over each figure's head was a set of earphones. But their faces—

Dusty had the eerie sensation that he had emerged from a world of human beings, and suddenly plunged down upon a make-believe planet. The face of each one of the strangely garbed figures was thin and pointed, to almost razor-blade thinness. Their eyes were not eyes really—more like glistening marbles set behind slitted skin. And the nose, rather than being a nose, was more like the peak or beginning of a receding forehead and jaw. The mouth was but another slit in the brown, blotched skin. And the hair—there was no hair showing beneath any one of the skull caps.

Fascinated, horrified, heart and brain filled with disgust, Dusty sat watching their bony hands flick up to the myriad of switches and plugs back of the cabinet doors. And to his clogged eardrums came a low murmur of inarticulate sound, whenever their lips moved.

"An interesting lot, aren't they, Captain?"

The words seemed to actually explode inside Dusty's head. Impulsively, he jerked about in his chair and gaped wide-eyed at a new weird spectacle.

Five men stood behind him. Each was tall, at least two or three inches taller than himself. They were clothed in neat-fitting black uniforms. On the left tunic front of each man was a tiny pair of spun gold wings, joined together in the center by a single bar of black onyx. In the center of each onyx was a tiny number in inlaid gold—the number 10.

Although the faces of the men in front of the wall cabinets

79

startled Dusty, the five faces he now gaped into startled him twice as much—not in the same eerie, horrified way, though. True, the faces were dark-skinned, almost a bronze and altogether fierce-looking. But the fact that dragged a gasp off Dusty's lips was their exact similarity. To look at one was to look at all five—identical in every detail. Each had the same large, hawkish nose, the same close-set, deep-sunken, jet black eyes, the same large mouth and the same coarse, ebony hair hanging raggedly down from under the black skull cap.

As Dusty gaped at them, his brain slowly awakened to life. And in that instant, memory in all its vividness came crashing back to him.

He let out a wild yell, and sprang to his feet, one hand automatically clawing for his holstered service gun. But his hand grasped at an empty holster, then dropped to his side in a gesture of savage helplessness. He had seen one of the five men dart forward a step, seen a queer-looking gun trained dead upon him. It was shaped like a tapering bulb, a tiny needle point in the tip. The back of it curved down to form a triggerless hand grip. Then its owner spoke. Harsh and rasping came the sound of his voice, even though the fang teeth showed in a wide smile.

"I've brought you back from the dead once, Captain. Are you going to force me to again? Don't you Americans ever know when you're beaten?"

DUSTY SHOOK his head, took a deep breath, and stood poised on the balls of his feet. What, where, how and when? There were so many questions he couldn't answer. He didn't try. He only knew that he was in the middle of some hell—a world he'd never get clear of, except by fighting. Let just one of them even try to lay a hand on him and he'd smash the hawkish face to a bloody pulp.

But a second later, as the man holding the queer gun spoke again, he realized the utter absurdity of his thoughts.

"Captain Ayres, your life has been in our hands for hours. It is still in our hands this very instant. One charge from this gas-gun which is trained on you, and you will drop like a suffocated fly. Can't you realize that we wish you no physical harm?"

Dusty bit his lower lip, stared intently at the man.

"Why?" he blurted out a moment later. "Why, damn you? You belong to the Black Invaders don't you?"

Like puppets they all bobbed their heads.

"Naturally," said the original speaker. "I was under the impression that you understood that quite thoroughly when we first met this afternoon. It was I, Captain, who talked with you."

The man bowed his head again. His smile broadened, and the corners of his mouth curled upward in a smirk of pride.

"The Black Hawk, eh?" Dusty mumbled in spite of himself. "And who are these others?"

"They?" echoed the man. "Well, to be truthful, Captain, each of them is the Black Hawk, when I find it necessary to make him such."

The Yank curbed the start the answer gave him. Then, for a reason he couldn't explain at the moment, he stepped close to the man and peered at him intently. When he stepped back, he was grinning.

"The Man of a Thousand Lives, eh?" he said. "I get the idea. But there *is* a difference. Yes, I'd recognize you the next time!"

Like a tiger who has been suddenly cornered, the man uttered a savage, grating sound. His eyes narrowed, and the veins in his temples went taut underneath the copper skin. Then, as quickly, he relaxed and shrugged.

"My compliments, Captain. I admit that others have noticed the difference, but it did them little good. To be sure, no more good than it will do you."

Dusty shrugged back at him casually, though he was now burning with curiosity. Life was still his, but he was in the center of an endless tangle of mystery. First—why was he alive? He put the question into words.

"And just why have you been so careful with my neck?"

"For various reasons, Captain," the Black Hawk replied. "In the first place, I wanted your plane, almost as much as I wanted you. In some things you Americans are quite clever. One of them is the manner in which you guard technical secrets of aircraft design. For some time we've known about the Silver Flash. We—"

"How the hell did you know it by name?" cried Dusty.

The other laughed.

"Good heavens, Captain, I know how to read! The name is painted on the nose of the plane, isn't it?"

A surging wave of bitter remorse swept over Dusty. The Silver Flash—his Silver Flash—in the hands of these devils.

"But, as I was saying," went on the harsh voice. "We failed in all of our attempts to get hold of the drawings for the plane.

As a matter of fact, we failed to learn anything, except what our eyes told us—and only then from a distance. So, we naturally took the trouble to get it intact. A very wonderful plane it is, too. Five years ahead of our latest Black Dart—the type plane you saw this afternoon, Captain."

The man stopped suddenly, and his black eyes fixed steadfastly on Dusty, and seemed to recede deeper into his head. They flashed tiny pin-points of white flame. A chilly tingling clutched at Dusty's heart, but he steeled himself outwardly and returned the steady glare.

"Yes, you are much more valuable to us alive than dead, Captain," the Black Hawk grated. "Else I would have killed you long before this. You see, you've cost me the lives of three pilots already."

Heart thumping with joy that he'd been of some use to his country's cause, the Yank nodded grimly.

"And there are ten thousand other Yank pilots who are just as good shots," he got out from between clenched teeth. "Most of them a damn sight better. So fire away. I'm just one of ten thousand. Paste that in your trick skull cap!

"But I'm still listening. Why save my hide? If it's because you think I may talk, then forget it. I'm an American, Black Hawk! A Yank—and if you don't know what that means, then you'll damned soon find out!"

Dusty stopped short as the other raised his hand in a soothing gesture.

"Of course you are an American, Captain," he said. "And a rather commendable example of the breed, I might add. Personally, I've always admired courage in friend and foe alike. But that is not the reason I've spared your life, and I did spare it, Captain.

"We could very easily have shot you down. Instead, we ringed you with a certain gas we've perfected. It's quite harmless, as regards the tissues of the body; it does not destroy life.

"Often times we wish to preserve the lives of those we conquer, so our chemical warfare department developed a gas that simply dulls the brain of its victim, and leaves him with nothing but a great craving for sleep. Perhaps you recall the sensation, but I rather doubt it. When we first tried it against the French, we found that they only recalled events up to the time they inhaled the fumes."

The man paused a moment to lick his lips, then continued like a professor delivering an oration.

"A MOST remarkable gas, Captain. With it we have captured countless prisoners for reconstruction work, and unlimited quantities of war supplies that would otherwise have been destroyed. Of course, when we want destruction we simply refrain from applying the restorative to the victim. Without it, he dies within twenty-four hours without once regaining consciousness.

"But in your case—well, Captain, we wanted you and your plane intact, so we acted accordingly. And by the way, you are in splendid condition, Captain. Your reaction to the restorative was quicker than that of any other man to whom I've ever seen it applied."

Eyes agate, Dusty simply stared at the man, while his brain

worked in a frantic effort to recall the details of a blank spot in his memory. But it was futile. It was as the Black Hawk had stated; he remembered everything from the time he left Dayton Field for Washington right up to when he'd first seen the greenish-brown web forming in the sky. But after that? He couldn't recall a thing.

"Thanks," he got out shortly. "But you haven't answered the question yet. You got the ship, but why save me?"

The Black Hawk smiled at him, pocketed his gas-gun.

"As a souvenir, Captain Ayres," came the astonishing reply. "Yours will be the honor of becoming the American Airman exhibit in our museum of war prisoners."

The Yank gulped, fought for words.

"W-what?" he finally managed to stammer out.

"Exactly what I said, Captain," returned the Black Hawk grimly. "Since we first began our conquering crusade, we have taken the first prisoner of each enemy nation, alive. As a matter of fact, we have taken a prisoner from each of the country's arms of defense. The collection is a sort of museum for the benefit of our own peoples. It gives them a certain sense of pride, boosts their morale when they see how many nationalities they have conquered and subdued. Yes, it's a custom originated by our great leader."

Dusty recoiled a step or two in spite of himself. A museum of war prisoners! God, what a devilish idea!

"You—you rotten dogs!" he blazed.

As the last word spilled off his lips, his brain flashed him a call of alarm. Instantly he ducked and twisted to the side. But the snarling black-uniformed figure charged like a flash of light. A hammerhead fist curved through the air, and caught Dusty flush on the side of his neck. His whole body went stiff as a board as he went crashing down on the floor.

The second impact released his momentarily paralyzed nerves, and he came bouncing up like a rubber ball. But that's as far as he got. Steel fingered hands gripped both his arms and pinned them to his sides. He struggled furiously, but the black pilots on either side of him had the strength of a dozen oxen.

Panting, cursing, Dusty returned the glare of the Black Hawk, who was standing straddle-legged in front of him.

"And it goes double for you, you tramp!" the Yank roared. "Call off these eggs and meet me man to man, if you dare. I'll knock you east of Suez!"

The Black Hawk's eyes retained their deadly gleam, but his tight lips curled back in a smirk.

"We've conquered you, Captain," he grated out. "But I see we have yet to subdue you. That, perhaps, will take time. But it shall be done, never fear. You were my choice in the beginning. What better than taking prisoner America's speed ace? And when by a stroke of good fortune you became involved in the initial stage of our capture of America, you doubled in importance to me.

"True, that fact added certain difficulties. It necessitated the risk of killing you, because of your increasing importance. But when we succeeded in luring you north of your country's border, the whole thing became quite simplified. So, all that remains now is the simple task of subduing you. And it shall be done."

"Think so?" Dusty blazed at him. "Well, try it, you black bum! You nailed me—I admit that. How you worked all those trick messages, how you jammed our ground stations with static, I don't know. But it's only the first trick, Black Hawk, and Uncle Sam has got a few of his own. You'll never lick us—never in God's world, do you hear? So do your damnedest with me—and to hell with you! That goes for your fancy murdering leader, Fire-Eyes, too!"

A light of stark madness and cruelty seeped into the other's eyes. Dusty knew that he was looking at certain death, that he was but inches away from it. But he didn't give a damn. His heart was deadened with the shame of his own blundering, his own failure in the hour of his country's greatest need. His brain was on fire, seething with a berserk desire to hurl himself at the smirking, copper-skinned rat in front of him.

"Call them off, Black Hawk!" he choked, as he got his breath. "Call them off, and let's see if you can take it, man to man!"

The other laughed in his face.

"You fool!" he said harshly. "You have courage but you are a fool. There were many interesting things I would have shown you, before I shipped you off to Fire-Eyes. But no, you shall not see them now. They would mean nothing to a fool. So take him away until he gets a little sense into that thick head of his, and mends his ways!"

The last was snapped at the two men who held Dusty. With a low growl they propelled him forward, toward a steel door. He struggled and fought, but he might just as well have tried holding back the tide.

Through the door he went, down a long, dimly-lighted hall, up a circular, steel stairway, and down another hall to a small door. As his guards paused in front of it, he made one last desperate effort to wrench himself free. He succeeded in getting one arm loose, and he drove his fist into the face of the other guard with every atom of his strength.

The man howled with pain, but did not let go. But before Dusty could jerk back his fist and slam it out again, a sledge hammer blow from behind knocked him off balance. The next thing he knew he was sprawling face down on a cold, stone floor, and above the buzzing in his ears came the slam of a metal door closing behind him. Even as he turned he heard the soft click of the bolt sliding into place.

WITH A groan he raised himself to his hands and knees, and remained that way for several minutes cursing softly to himself. Then eventually he turned over, sat up and looked about him.

There was not a great deal to see.

He was in a small room, about ten by ten and eight feet high The walls and the ceiling were of steel plating, and the floor was of solid stone. Against the right wall was an army cot with a single blanket, no pillow. Against the left wall was a bare, narrow table. At the back wall was a smaller table with a towel, a small basin and a pitcher of water on top of it. In front of him, was a five foot by three foot steel door, with what looked like a hinged section at the bottom. The light in the room came from a single, screened-over bulb sunk up into the middle part of the ceiling.

"Dusty Ayres, the prize sap! So what?"

The sound of his own voice startled him, sent his nerves tingling. He laughed bitterly and got to his feet.

"So what?" he echoed thickly to himself. "Well, wash up for one thing. Yeah make yourself nice and pretty and maybe they'd give you a special niche in the prisoners' museum, you block-headed dummy!"

Weaving over to the rear table, he splashed water into the basin, then doused his hands and face in it as best he could, and dried them on the towel. That helped a lot. The cold water cleared his head, eased the throbbing pain, and served to take some of the bitter sting of self resentment from his heart. After all, why jump down your own neck? It wasn't going to help. Forget it, and think of how the hell one could get out of this place.

With a resigned shrug he walked over to the bed, threw himself upon it and tried to segregate the twisted thoughts in his brain. But the result was like running around in a circle, and ending up right where he started. The blank spots skipped him every time.

In the first place, where was he? What time was it? His watch had been taken away from him. And with a start he realized that he hadn't seen a single window. Every room or hall he'd been in had been windowless, like the one he was in now. Where was the Silver Flash? How his hands ached to be gripping the control stick. Hell, what a laugh that was! Would he ever see the old bus again?

He moaned aloud and fought back the tears of helpless rage that crowded to his eyes. What a fool he'd been. His C.O. had picked him for the honor. General Horner had entrusted him with an important mission—counted on him, and he'd failed. Yes, he'd let his own gang down, his C.O., General Horner, and his country.

Hell, he'd tried. But he'd been tricked, completely fooled. Perhaps any other of Uncle Sam's eagles would have been tripped up the same way. But the fact remained that he was the one. God knew what might be happening now while he sat here eating his heart out between steel walls. Damn it, he had to do something!

But his own thought echoed back to mock him—do *what?*

There was no answer to that. Struggling to keep his sanity he lay there on the army cot, going over every conceivable detail in his mind, and getting nowhere. Dusty Ayres, speed ace of Uncle Sam's fighting eagles, was sunk—sunk deeper than hell. For all the good he was to his country, he might just as well be a thousand feet below the international meteorological station at either the north or south pole.

How long he lay there battling with his thoughts, he didn't know. There was no way of telling time. Suddenly he heard a clicking noise. Like a flash he sat up, trying to place the sound. It came from the other side of the steel door.

As he stared at the door, he saw the hinged part at the bottom open inward, and a tray of food was slid into the room. For an instant he got a glimpse of a bony hand holding the tray, then the hand disappeared and the trap clicked shut.

The hope that had flickered to life in Dusty died out again. Hell yes, museum prisoners had to be fed, didn't they? Well, as far as he was concerned, they could take their damn food and stuff it down their own throats. He'd starve before he'd touch a bit of it. With a savage curse he rolled over on his stomach.

But regardless of the situation, a man's empty stomach has a most pronounced way of making its owner acutely conscious of its presence. And Dusty Ayres was no exception to the rule. For ten minutes he doggedly stuck it out. Then as the savory flavor of soup and meat filled his nostrils, he weakened enough to roll over and stare at the tray. Another five minutes and he sat up. Five minutes more and he went over to the tray, convinced that he really should eat. He needed his strength, that was the only reason. It wasn't that he was hungry. Hell no, but perhaps it would be a darn good idea to eat this one meal. There was no telling when he would get another.

Picking up the tray, he placed it on the wall table and pulled the cot over for a chair. Grudgingly, he admitted to himself that the soup was good. It was tomato and rice, and he sure liked rice!

He'd almost finished, when suddenly, he stopped a spoonful half way to his mouth and stared at it. It was not all soup and rice in the spoon. There was something else—a tiny white square. It was like a piece of paper that had been wadded together. He picked it out and started to toss it on the tray when his hand froze and his eyes went wide. There was not the slightest doubt. The white square was wadded paper.

Dropping the spoon into the bowl, he unfolded the wad with trembling fingers, and presently smoothed it out to an inch and one half of soggy white paper. A gasp choked in his throat as he saw a jumble of black dots on its surface. But they meant nothing to him.

There was a short row at the top, and a long row at the bottom. Both rows were made up of little squares of dots, so it seemed. Yet as he studied them closely he saw that they weren't all squares.

Frowning, he turned the paper over. It was blank on the other side. Then he turned it back, and studied the dots again. A split second later he almost cried out aloud.

In turning it back he had turned it so that now the long line was on top and the short line on the bottom. The squares were no longer squares—the dots pinpricked in the paper formed words and figures. Hardly able to believe his eyes, he read:

YOUR CHIN UP YANK10 OF X34

CHAPTER 8
TRAPPED!

LIKE A drowning man clutching at a lifeline, Dusty clutched at the tiny, mysterious ray of hope that the message sent flashing through him. 10 of X34? At the moment he didn't know, nor particularly care. The one truth that pounded through his brain was that some person, unknown to him, knew that he was here. And that person was calling upon him to keep courage. God be praised—he was not alone among enemies. Somewhere in this eerie maze of steel rooms and hallways, there was a friend. A friend who might get him out.

The rest of the food on the tray was forgotten. Eyes riveted to the quivering paper he held, he studied every bit of it with savage fierceness. But the one message he had read was all that it contained. For the moment it was enough.

Like the waters of a flood tide rushing into an empty bay, strength and hope surged back to him. In a matter of seconds, he had been lifted from the hell-pit of despair and borne up to the peak heights of renewed courage and faith. True, it was but a mysterious lifeline flung to him as he floundered helplessly, but it was something.

"10 of X34?" he murmured in breathless wonderment, "who the devil? X34 means Horner, of course, but how could he know I'm—?"

The rest was left unfinished as a whistling gasp rippled off his lips. Ten? Did Ten mean Agent 10—the foreign agent General Horner had counted on—the man whose last teletype message was never finished? No! Hell no, it couldn't. That man was probably dead. And even if he was still alive, he was over in Europe, thousands of miles away. He—

Dusty stiffened and sat with mouth agape, as a new thought came to him. God Almighty, he didn't know where he was, himself. The Black Hawk had said that his life had been in their hands for hours. How many hours had passed since he'd seen that gas web hanging in the sky? Where was he? He could be most any place, America or Europe, or maybe on the moon, for all that.

With an impulsive movement he crushed the paper to a wad and placed both doubled fists against his temples.

"Hold it, kid, hold it!" he grated at himself. "It looks like you've got a break, but don't go haywire!"

With a great effort he got hold of his jangled nerves. Then with calm deliberation he tore the soggy paper into tiny bits, put the bits in his mouth and washed them down with a spoonful of soup.

Hardly had he done that than the lock on the door snapped back and the door swung open. The Black Hawk and a cruel-looking guard stood on the threshold. The Black's eyes fastened on Dusty's in fierce concentration. For almost five seconds the tableau remained motionless then, slowly, the Black Hawk walked into the room, the guard at his heels clutching a gas-gun in his huge paw.

Steeling himself, the Yank rose to his feet and forced a grin to his lips.

"And so what now?" he got out lightly. "Figure to shoot your face off some more?"

The other didn't speak. With a quick step he went up to the table, bent over the tray of food, and peered at it intently. A moment later he took a spoon and carefully prodded the contents of the various dishes.

"Say, what's the idea?" snapped Dusty. "If you want the damned stuff, take it."

The Black Hawk said something in a language Dusty didn't understand. The next thing he knew, the guard had pinned him up against the wall and was searching him thoroughly. He started to struggle, then suddenly changed his mind and stood motionless until the man had finished.

As the guard shook his head at his superior, the Black Hawk muttered a curse, snatched up the gas-gun and leveled it at Dusty.

"Where is it?"

The words echoed sharply against the steel walls. Dusty shrugged.

"Where's what?"

"The message concealed in your food, Captain," said the other with deadly evenness. You've been watched every second. One of my men saw you take something out of your food. He said it was a folded slip of paper. Where is it, Captain?"

Inwardly the Yank's heart looped over with excitement and relief. Thank God he'd swallowed the message in time. Outwardly his expression was one of blank amazement.

"What in hell are you talking about?" he stalled. "Who saw who with a folded slip of paper? You're crazy!"

The Black Hawk smiled nastily, and the muscles about his jaws tightened. With a sudden movement he went up to the rear wall.

"Look here, Captain!"

PLACING THE flat of his hand against the steel wall, at a point in the center and about a foot from the ceiling, he twisted sharply to the right. Then he took his hand away. Dusty gulped and stared. Where a second before there had been a solid sheet of steel, there was now a tiny slit, about four inches long and a quarter of an inch wide.

"A little slide panel," came the Black Hawk's voice, "that enables the guard to watch the actions of the man in this detention cell. It is also part of the ventilation system. But the point is, Captain, that you have been watched. We wouldn't want our first American prisoner to become too remorseful and try to commit suicide, you know. And the guard reports that you took a piece of paper out of your soup, and read something written upon it!"

As the man spoke, he moved close to Dusty and raised the gas-gun until its muzzle was on the level with the Yank's eyes. At the same time the guard pinned Dusty's hands behind his back.

"You remember my words, Captain?" the Black pilot purred, nodding toward the gas-gun. "Just one small charge from this and you drop like a dead fly. Where is that paper?"

The Yank's blood ran cold, but he kept his face expressionless and his eyes riveted on the other.

"You're crazy, Black Hawk!" he grated. "There wasn't any paper!"

"So you swallowed it, eh?" the man shot right back. "Well, in that case, you'd have to tell us what it said."

Dusty was surprised at the chuckle that spiked from his own lips.

"Yeah?" he got out. "Well, that's something else you can try and do. Even if there had been a paper, I'd see you in hell first, before I'd tell you."

"Brave words, Captain! But death is not pleasant—not this kind of death. I understand that the membranes shrivel up and the lungs contract, finally the heart explodes. Most unpleasant,

Captain, I assure you of that. Now, what did that paper say, and who signed it?"

Though death seemed to be reaching out at him, something in the back of Dusty's head told him that it would not touch him. The Black Hawk had kept him alive too long as it was, to kill him now. The man was playing the old prisoner-bluff game, and playing it to the limit.

"What it said, oh?" Dusty echoed. "Is that what you want to know? Well, I'll tell you."

As Dusty paused, the Black's lips slid back in an eager, triumphant leer.

"Yes, yes, Captain, that's what I want!"

"It said," replied the Yank slowly. "Merry Xmas from Santa Claus!"

For a second the Black Hawk's jaw dropped in blank astonishment. Then the features of his cruel face twisted with rage and his sunken eyes virtually spewed tongues of flame. With a hideous shriek he lashed out with his free hand. Unable to protect himself, Dusty could only jerk his head to one side and take the savage blow on his left shoulder. But even then the pain brought a groan to his lips.

"Go ahead, you rat!" he rasped from between clenched teeth. "Keep it up. Get in your innings. But some day I'll give you two for one. Yeah, even if I have to wait for you in hell to do it. And that's a promise, so help me!"

But the Black Hawk didn't strike again. Instead, he stepped back a pace, stood there glaring savagely at his prisoner. Then gradually the anger faded from his eyes, and to Dusty's amazement he smiled and raised his hand in a half salute.

"My apologies, Captain," he said. "Of course I was mistaken. Not even a fool hero would face certain death, and joke as you did. But about that promise you gave me. I accept it with pleasure, and I hope that the day will come when you can try to make it come true. But I doubt it. In time, you will be sent to a place from whence there is no return. I do not mean death, for death is the least of punishments that we Black Invaders can inflict."

The man paused, nodded again.

"And now, I leave you for the present," he said, moving toward the door and bobbing his head at the guard. "If there is anything you wish, simply call out. Your watcher, back of that wall, will convey your wishes to me."

With that the Black Hawk and the guard ducked out through the steel door. Seconds later the lock bolt clicked into place and Dusty was alone again.

For several minutes he stood still, staring dully at the door. Then with a stifled moan he went over to the cot, sat down, and buried his head in his hands. Within him rose up a seething tempest of fear, disappointment and bitter chagrin. A spark of hope in a world of mystery had now faded out. The Black Hawk had lied when he'd said he was mistaken. From now on the food would be searched, and perhaps 10 of X34 would be trapped. God, he, Dusty, was not only responsible for his own doom, but probably the cause of doom for another Yank. He wished he'd never been born.

"CAPTAIN AYRES!" Like a man who has been awakened out of deep slumber by some peculiar sound that penetrated his dulled senses, Dusty jerked his head up and frowned into space.

Then he heard it again, a low, hissing whisper.

"Captain Ayres! Here—the rear wall!"

A tremor of electrified action sliced through him. He started to his feet and walked quickly over to the rear wall. The panel slide was open, and behind it he could faintly see the whites of gleaming eyes. He placed both hands against the wall and kept his eyes raised toward the slit.

"Who are you?" he breathed.

"Agent 10," came the faint reply. "Will that wash stand hold you? You've got to get close to this crack. Try it!"

Fighting desperately to keep his hands steady, Dusty pulled the table over, tried his weight on it. The wooden legs creaked a bit, but the table seemed strong enough. Climbing up on it, he braced himself in a half crouched position and put his lips close to the slit. He started to whisper something, then suddenly changed his mind.

"Agent 10?" he said. "Never heard of him."

"Don't be a damned fool!" hissed the other. "This isn't a trick."

Dusty scowled. A queer sensation was surging through him. He couldn't tell whether it was a sensation of joy or caution. In the light of past events, he was prepared to expect almost anything. He put the question slowly.

"How do I know?"

"You don't!" came the startling surprise. "But damn it, man, you've got to believe me!"

An idea suddenly came to Dusty.

"Wait a second!" he breathed. "If you're Agent 10, tell me this—what was the last message you sent on the teletype, and to whom?"

There followed a few seconds of quivering silence, then the man on the other side of the wall spoke again.

"To Horner, X34. I started to tell him where Fire-Eyes was reported to have gone in a high speed bomber. But I couldn't finish the message. I—"

"Check, old man!" Dusty cut in excitedly. "But what happened? How did you get here? Where the hell are we anyway?"

"Shut up, and let me talk, Ayres!" the other breathed back fiercely. "You didn't tell them about that note in the soup, did you?"

"No. But they suspect. The guard who was where you are now saw me reading it."

"That's okay," was the dumbfounding reply. "I was that guard. I told the Black Hawk I'd seen you read a message. I—"

"You?" gasped Dusty, as his head whirled. "But what the—?"

"Building myself up with him, you dope! Now he thinks I'm a real bright-eyes, and has given me the job of watching you for the rest of the night."

"Night?" echoed the Yank in Blaring. "What night? What time is it, anyway? I don't know what the hell this is all—"

"It's almost midnight of Wednesday," was the reply. "You've been here since yesterday afternoon. Now, shut up, don't interrupt, and let me talk. Just keep your eyes on the door. If the lock moves, rap the wall once, and then get down off the table. Got it?"

Dusty nodded, then realized his ear was jammed against the crack. He turned his head.

"Right, 10! Let her rip!"

Ear jammed again to the crack, and eyes riveted to the door, Dusty waited with tingling nerves for the other to speak. There was a long pause then softly whispered words began to pour into his ear.

"Listen, Ayres, I don't know just where we are, but I'm pretty sure it's some place in Ontario, Canada. And here's why. As I was finishing my last message to Horner, a mopping-up squad of Blacks got too close to me. I'm supposed to be in their army, but if they'd spotted me with the teletype key, it would have been curtains. So I destroyed it and beat it."

"Transport planes of Black troops were leaving the Paris area, and in the confusion I managed to get aboard one. Twelve hours later we landed. It was dark and I didn't know where I was. An officer took a squad of us and marched us into a shaft in the side of a hill. That's where we are now—in the middle of a range of hills. I haven't been able to get out because it's a two man job. There are too many guards. But I've found this out. The Blacks have been building this place for months. It's a combination air base and signal base."

THE VOICE paused for a moment, and Dusty grabbed the opportunity to ask one of the million odd questions that were coursing through his brain.

"Couldn't you see where the transport was going?"

"No," came the answer. "There were no cabin windows. But I know we swung north for a long time and then veered toward the south, because it got cold as hell and then eased off. Since I've been here I've overheard a couple of these rat officers talking. From what they said I place this spot a couple of hundred miles north of Lake Superior. It's in Ontario some place, because I've heard them mention the name several times.

"But, here's the point, Ayres. This is their main power signal station on the North American continent. Remember that big room you were in? I saw you there. That's the central control room. Every one of those cabinet relays contact with a hidden wave-length station in the United States, a Black agent station, see?

"In that way they can set up a magnetic disturbance in any section of the country and blanket-out our stations. That's what they've been doing for two days. The whole of the United States is static jammed right from this spot here. Get the idea?"

"Partly," breathed Dusty. "But what's that get them in the long run? They jam up their own communications, don't they?"

"That's just the point!" came the hissing answer. "It doesn't matter because their plans are obviously all ready made. They are jamming our stations so that we can't contact each other, and in the meantime they are sending out fake orders over the U.S. government wave-lengths to our battle squadrons and air fleets. They can do that right from here—clear the air long enough to get their fake message through and then jam it before there is a call back for confirmation. My God, Ayres, they've sent almost the entire Atlantic fleet chasing down to defend the Canal. And—"

"I heard part of that order!" cut in Dusty breathlessly. "I heard that the Canal was destroyed. How—?"

"It was destroyed two days ago! They did it with a couple of radio-controlled bombers from their Pacific fleet. Crashed them into two of the locks. I know that much, definitely."

"But why send our fleet down there, if they've already destroyed the Canal?" Dusty asked excitedly. "Hell, of course, I get it—to leave our East Coast open to attack!"

For a moment there was nothing but silence beyond the steel wall. A pang of sudden fear sliced through Dusty.

"Hey, 10, did you hear me? Are you still there?"

"Yes, I hear you. But I don't know where they plan to attack—I mean attack with a landing force."

"But it's obvious that they plan to take the East Coast!" Dusty cut in. "With the fleet headed south, New York and Philly are left wide open. And, say, I heard another of their fake messages. One ordering most of our central states air squadrons to the West Coast."

"You did?" the other hissed. "When was that?"

Dusty told him in a few rapid-fire sentences of what happened during his flight up the West Coast. As he finished there came a low groan from beyond the slit.

"Even the ground wires, too, eh?" echoed Agent 10. "God, that's the one thing I'd been hoping against. But I should have realized they would. The devils are clever. They think of everything, curse their hides!"

The silence that followed the last remark fired Dusty with a frantic desire for action. Action—anything, rather than remain cooped up here in the bottom of a hill. The news he had received from Agent 10 created a reaction of liquid fire which soured through his veins. There were still a few blank spots, but he could fill those in from his imagination. The important thing was that Black high-speed bombers, transports, and pursuit planes were already on the North American continent!

He jammed his lips to the crack.

"We've got to do something, 10!" he hissed fiercely. "We've got to get word to Washington somehow. Damn it, man, the East Coast is wide open. We've got—"

"Hold it, Ayres, hold it! There's something else we must do first. Listen—as long as this power station functions, the U.S. is just banging around in the dark. Merely getting word to Washington won't help much. It would still be impossible to contact our defense units and countermand the fake orders. I doubt if there'd even be time for courier contact work.

"That leaves us with just one possible move. It will probably mean curtains for us both. But hell, we're Yanks, and we've got to risk it. At least, I'll risk it. How about you, Ayres?"

Dusty's face went grim with savage determination.

"What do *you* think, Agent 10?" he grated. "Shoot! What's to be done?"

"Just this—destroy this power station. If we can, it frees the air for our stations."

"Okay!" whispered Dusty, his heart pounding against his ribs. "That suits me swell. But how the devil am I going to get out of this room?"

"Leave that to me," came the answer. "Now listen, Ayres—"

The voice paused, and when it spoke again Dusty had to strain his eardrum to catch it.

"Remember the word, 'static.' When you hear that word again, you'll know it's me. Then use your own judgment about what will follow. Remember, when you hear static, be ready for action. Now, get down and finish that food. Make believe you're eating, if you don't want it. And keep your chin up, Yank!"

Something clicked in Dusty's ear. He turned, started to whisper a question, but stopped. The panel had slid back in place and he was looking at nothing but a blank steel wall. For a moment he hesitated, then with a shrug, he climbed down off the wash stand, moved it over to its proper place, and seated himself on the cot.

AUTOMATICALLY, HE ate some of the meat, but he didn't even notice its savory flavor. His brain was spinning over too fast with what had just happened to register anything else.

For the first time in years, it seemed to him, a glad song was in his heart. He felt like a man whom fate has pulled back from the very lip of the grave. What lay ahead didn't matter.

Though he had no absolute proof of the man's true identity, something deep down inside of him told him to put his faith in the owner of that whispering voice. Damn it, the man couldn't be anybody else but Agent 10. He just couldn't be—he knew too many of the important details.

Subconsciously he wondered what the man looked like. Was he tall or short, fat or thin, young or old? A member of the Black Army, eh? What a man! What things his eyes must have looked upon! The Blacks were clever? Well, there was one Yank who was going them one better.

A sudden surge of pride flooded through Dusty. What a man to know—what a man to work with!

The last stuck in his brain. Work with? Agent 10 hadn't said anything about the details of his plan. He'd simply said, "Leave it to me. Remember the word, static." Just words, and what did they mean? The man had admitted that the place was well guarded. How did he expect to get him out of this steel-walled room? And suppose he did, then what? The Blacks would spot his uniform a block away.

He raised his eyes and stared dully at the wall. But he wasn't seeing the wall before him. He was seeing the steel corridors through which the guards had rushed him, the circular flight of stairs and the big, long room with its cabinet-covered walls. The control room—the very heart of the static web the Blacks had spread over the United States.

Sitting there, picturing that room, a strange sensation seeped through him. This all seemed unbelievable, like something he was reading out of a story book. From that room, deep down in the bowels of a hill range, a victory-thirsting brain was stifling American air communication. One nerve center was able to plunge a great nation into a void of mystery.

It was fantastic. During his lifetime, science had done wonders with the invisible power man called electricity. But, anything like this? No. Not once during his time spent at the Air Force War College at Dayton had any such offensive or defensive tactic been spoken of. True, he'd learned how it was possible to static jam a single station with planted, high-powered transformers. You simply left the transmitter key open. But to be able to static jam any and all stations, regardless of their distance from the central point? Well—

Dusty left the thought unfinished. It was beyond him, outside the limits of his training. But it nevertheless chilled him to the core as he realized the propensities of the menace his country was facing. A blood-thirsting horde of destroyers, yet geniuses in their own right.

Wide awake to the danger that confronted them, fully prepared to meet it when it struck, the American people had been practically crippled and cut off from each other in one lightning swoop. The key defense cut off in a flash. If the Black Invaders could accomplish that stroke while they were still subduing Europe, what hellish things would they do once they got a firm foothold on American grounds?

The Yank pilot shivered in spite of himself. There was no use thinking about it. War was here! It had already slashed down with terrorizing brutality. This was no time to indulge in gruesome speculation of the future. The important thing was to act—to act now, and let come what may take care of itself.

To act, now! The thought was like a saw-toothed blade twisting in his brain. God, he could do absolutely nothing now. His task was to wait and keep his chin up. Wait? It seemed as though he'd been waiting since the beginning of time.

Suddenly his heart turned over as he heard the lock bolt in the steel door clicked back. Agent 10? Yes, thank—But as he turned, his heart went cold. The door swung open and the Black Hawk stood on the threshold. Behind him was a guard, evil-eyed and leering menacingly.

Curbing the disappointment in his heart, the Yank gave the Black Hawk a fleeting glance, and turned back to his food.

"Don't you like our food, Captain? Or is it your custom to eat slowly?"

Dusty said nothing, and kept his head bent over the plate lest the other have the satisfaction of seeing the strained look that he knew must be stamped on his face.

"Maybe it's because you've been too busy reading more messages you've found?"

The chuckle that accompanied the words stung Dusty, like raw salt in an open wound. For one crazy second he had a reckless desire to slap a plate square into the Black's face. But he killed the idea the instant it came to him. Instead he turned and eyed the man steadily.

"I'm your prisoner, Black Hawk!" he gritted. "And that makes you top man. But I don't have to talk to you, see? So save your breath and go crowing up another alley. In other words, you waste my time. You might just as well go ask questions of somebody who'll answer them."

The Black Hawk stepped close to him. There was a smile on his big mouth, but seething anger in his sunken eyes.

"You're beginning to annoy me, Captain," he said. "I saved

your life and I've treated you with the courtesy afforded important prisoners. But you deem it fit to act otherwise. The guard told me that you were not eating, so I decided to come here, personally, and find out what was wrong. I don't do that always. But you interest me, greatly. However, I see you want a different sort of treatment. So you shall have it!"

With that the Black nodded at the guard. The result was, that before he knew what was happening, Dusty was spilled from his chair and sent flying up against the opposite wall. A red haze filmed before his eyes as he scrambled to his feet.

"Why, you damned—"

He got no further. With the speed of flickering light the guard leaped backward and to the side, so that the Black Hawk was between them. And as he moved one word spilled off his lips.

"Static!"

Stunned, Dusty stood rooted to the spot while his whirling brain tried frantically to whip action orders to his paralyzed muscles.

CHAPTER 9
AGENT TEN

"STATIC, AYRES, static!"

As the voice called out again, a spring inside Dusty was suddenly released. He leaped forward as the guard hurled himself onto the Black Hawk.

The man spun and tried to jerk up the gas-gun clenched in

his right hand, but the guard's blow knocked it free and sent it skidding across the stone floor. And at that moment Dusty's clenched fist connected with solid jaw bone.

A gasp whistled out of the wide lips, and the Black Hawk crashed down, with the other two on top of him.

"His mouth, Ayres! Gag it! I'll take his arms and legs."

Brain functioning at full speed, Dusty didn't waste a second. He jammed his handkerchief into the Black Hawk's mouth, ripped off his service tie, and bound the gag in place. By that time the guard had jack-knifed the Hawk's arms and legs and lashed them together with his belt.

Then the guard rolled the Black over, face to the floor, and sat on the small of the man's back. His leering features wrinkled into a grin.

"And that's that! Nice work, Ayres. Kind of took you off guard, though, didn't it?"

Dusty fought for control of his tongue, and stared pop-eyed into the grinning, but horrible face.

"Y-yeah!" he managed a moment later. "But good God, man, your—"

"Face?" finished the other. "Hell, how'd you expect me to look—like a Yank soldier? Makeup's a big part of my job, you know."

A shaky laugh spilled off Dusty's lips.

"I'll say it is!" he breathed. "But—"

He stopped short, darted over and scooped up the gas-gun. A glance showed him the clamp trigger in the grip, and a sense of security flooded through him.

"Come on, 10, let's get out. What's the next move?" And as the other remained seated, "Come on, for God's sake, we can't stay here very much longer!"

Agent 10 nodded and gestured.

"Yes we can, Ayres," he said. "And we're going to. So take it easy, and get your breath."

Dusty gaped at him in amazement, and for one fleeting second the clammy fingers of fear clutched at his heart.

"Why?" he blurted out. "I don't understand!"

The secret agent grinned.

"But I do," he said, almost casually. "We've got to stay here for ten more minutes. The place we're headed for is occupied right now. It's a room downstairs. To try to take it by storm would be asking for suicide before we even got started. But it's ten of two now. At 2:00 o'clock the room will be empty. Then will be our chance, if any."

Dusty glanced at the rear wall, then looked meaningfully at Agent 10. The man shook his head.

"No one there," he spoke quietly. "That's supposed to be my post. I simply left it and reported to Black Hawk that you weren't eating. I was hoping he'd come down here and order me along with him. Well, I got the break. And here we are."

"But how about somebody missing him?" Dusty insisted, as the frenzied desire for action burned hotter within him. "Suppose some of the others come in here?"

"They wouldn't dare, in the first place," was the reply. "He," pointing a finger at the prostrate man under him, "would kill the first man who came strutting in without knocking. And if anybody does knock, I'll simply order them the hell away. Or else let them in, and treat them accordingly."

The poise of the man filled Dusty with admiration. Agent 10 acted as though he were enjoying a pleasant drawing-room conversation. A perpetual smile was on his lips, and his every movement was one of calm deliberation. He seemed to have no nerves at all. Dusty heaved a sigh and sat down on the edge of the cot.

"You win, fellow!" he exclaimed. "I've heard of men with guts, but, boy, you cop all the medals!"

"Forget it, Ayres!" snorted the other. "I've just been living and eating with these rats for almost three years. You forget what might happen to you after a while. But you're no sissy yourself, lad. The way you stood up to this egg with a gas-gun in your face, and told him where to head in—well, that's one for the book too, Ayres.

"But listen, while we're waiting, tell me what you've been doing. Some kind of a contact flight, wasn't it? At least that's what I gathered. On my chiefs orders, wasn't it?"

DUSTY NODDED, hesitated a moment, and then with sudden decision he gave the secret agent a detailed account of his experiences. The man listened in thoughtful silence. At times he frowned, at others smiled faintly, but at no time did he interrupt. Even when the pilot had finished, Agent 10 remained seated, chin in hand, staring dully at the floor.

Presently he took his hand away from his chin, doubled it into a fist and pounded it softly against the palm of his other hand.

"I don't get it," he muttered savagely. "I don't get it at all. Fire-Eyes would be a fool to try to attack New York. He knows damned well that our coast defenses would blow him to hell and back. Of course, he could smash up the city a bit with his radio-controlled bombers. But to land troops? He wouldn't stand a chance. He certainly must realize that. Yet, perhaps that's his idea, after all. The man's insane with his own power."

"Say," Dusty cut in, "I just happened to remember—that last message to Horner. You started to say that Fire-Eyes was reported heading some place in a high speed bomber, but you didn't finish it. The message was blocked out on the machine."

"Oh, that?" the other echoed. "That was a rumor I heard. He was supposed to be heading for Bermuda where his Atlantic fleet is at anchor. But later I heard he'd gone back into Central Asia. He could be any place, now; for all I know."

Dusty leaned forward excitedly.

"Perhaps here?" he breathed.

The secret agent started to laugh and shake his head, but he checked himself and frowned. Then with a muttered curse he shrugged.

"Your guess is as good as mine, Ayres. He may be here, but I don't think so. The Black Hawk seems to be in complete command, and he sure wouldn't be if Fire-Eyes was around."

"Listen," spoke up Dusty quickly. "Just what the hell is this place, and why couldn't you get out? If it's in Canada, why haven't the Canadian authorities spotted it? It just doesn't read right, if you get what I mean."

"I get you all right, Ayres. But you don't know the Blacks

like I do. Sometimes I almost think they're a bunch of phantoms. You can't figure what they're going to do five minutes ahead. They're absolutely uncanny. Hell, you could go to sleep at night, and wake up and find them in your hair.

"But as I said before, I don't know for sure where we are. I only know that we're twelve hours by plane away from Paris. And as you were brought down on the North Dakota border line, it's only logical to suppose that we're in Canada. Besides, since I've been here I've heard these beasts talking about how long it took them to build this place, heard them mention Ontario, and that this is their central power station and air base on the North American continent."

"But why haven't you been able to get out?" insisted Dusty as the other paused. "Maybe a look at the countryside would—"

"Right! But this room where we are right now is four flights down. The only way out is either by the stairs, or in an elevator at the far end of the corridor. A certain number of Blacks are assigned to each of the five floors, and their orders are to stay on that floor. Luckily, I was given a guard job that permitted me to go around on the three bottom floors.

"As a matter of fact, if I hadn't got that job I probably would never have known you were here. But to try and get out without a signed pass from the Black Hawk—well, just no can do. Besides, I've been too interested in that central control room downstairs to try to get out. Before I leave here, that room's going to be a heap of junk, or I just don't leave!"

There was a moment's silence and then Dusty spoke again.

"I hate to keep asking a lot of dumb questions," he said. "But

I've got an idea, and—well, I'm just trying to get as much of the picture as I can."

The other shrugged, glanced at his watch.

"That's okay, Ayres. Shoot. You've got four minutes left."

"IT'S ABOUT my being here," said Dusty. "I wonder how they brought me, and where my ship is now. God, it gripes me to think they've got that bus."

"My guess is that you came by air," replied Agent 10. "In either this hill or the next one there is a subterranean drome. There must be one with the Black Hawk being around here. Incidentally, did you notice his wings—the figure ten? Well, that's the crack air unit of the Black Invaders. If you live to meet any of them again, don't give them a single break. They're a bunch of killers."

Dusty's eyes went hard.

"Don't worry," he grated, "I won't! But you spoke of a room downstairs. What is it? And what's your plan of action? Give me the worst, Agent 10. I can take it, I reckon."

The other pursed his lips and stared at his bony hands a moment.

"That room," he began presently, "is the power room. It contains the controls for every bit of electrical power used in this place. I was only able to get one quick glimpse at it last night. Up to then I didn't even know what it was. If we succeed in smashing all the stuff in that room we'll put the central control on the bum for a long time to come. And that will mean that this crowd here will be unable to jam any of our government wave-lengths, or even send out messages of their own, except by the old-time wireless method."

"I get you," cut in Dusty eagerly. "But why couldn't they

repair the damage we do? Rebuild it, I mean. Would it take them long?"

"Plenty long," nodded Agent 10. "If I know anything about electricity, and what will happen, it wouldn't be worth their while. You see, they are not only using standard high-tension current here, but they're tapping the cosmic system as well. By shorting the two systems, we'll melt every damned wire and plug they've got in the place. Yeah, if you've ever wondered what hell-fire looks like, you're going to find out firsthand.

"Well, let's go, Ayres. They switch over to standard current at two and keep it that way for five hours, so that the cosmic generator can bring the charging cells up to maximum power. I just noticed the light flickering, and that means they've switched over and have locked up the room for the five-hour period. So, come on, and do just as I say."

Like a man who had suddenly decided to take a short stroll before turning in, Agent 10 got to his feet and leisurely flexed his muscles. Then he bent over the prostrate Black Hawk, shoved a hand into the pilot's pocket and pulled out a key ring. He grinned at Dusty.

"Save us the trouble of smashing down doors, and maybe waking somebody up," he said. "Now stay right behind me, and keep that gas-gun ready. If I yell, don't be afraid to use it. And one more thing, Ayres, as soon as we've wrecked the place, it'll be every man for himself. The place will be a raging hell. Try and get out, if you can, and get word to Washington of what you know, see?"

Dusty swallowed hard and nodded.

"Sure, but what about you?"

"I'll take care of myself," came the quiet answer. "No matter what happens, my job is with the Black Invaders, yours with the Yanks. We're both working toward the same goal. Okay, here we go."

Selecting one of the keys, Agent 10 slid it into a key groove in the door and twisted slowly. The lock-bolt clicked back and the door swung open. Motioning for Dusty to stay right where he was, the man slipped outside. A thousand minutes of fear and doubt dragged by, then his head reappeared in the doorway and with finger to his lips he nodded an okay signal.

Steeling himself against the qualms and tremors which rippled through him, Dusty gripped the gas-gun in one hand, bunched the other fist, and stepped through the doorway.

Hugging the steel wall of the corridor, Dusty stuck close behind Agent 10 as they edged toward the circular staircase twenty yards away. It seemed to Dusty that they would never reach it. The small of his back itched unbearably, and though he didn't dare look behind, he had the feeling that thousands of cruel black eyes were glued on him.

Two feet from the stairs, Agent 10 went rigid. Dusty's heart looped over and spun down inside of him. The scuffing sound of footsteps blasted against his ears. Someone was coming up the stairs.

A moment later the head and shoulders of a big Black guard came into view. The man glanced at Agent 10 and started to nod when his fierce eyes fastened on Dusty. His right hand streaked to his tunic pocket and his big mouth commenced to open. But not a sound came out from between his thick lips. Agent 10's gas-gun came up like a flash and Dusty saw the thin stream of purple smoke mush into the guard's face. The guard stiffened and toppled forward. With his free arm Agent 10 caught him, eased him to the floor, then nodded at Dusty.

"Gotta run for it!" he hissed. "Stick close!"

Even as the words swished out of his mouth, Agent 10 was turning the corner and racing light-footed down the circular stairs. Heart pounding against his ribs, Dusty stuck right with him. The faint patter of their footsteps seemed to crash through the silence like the staccato yammering of Browning guns.

But Agent 10 didn't pause for a single instant. As soon as he reached the landing below he turned left along the corridor, dashed down its entire length and cut sharply to the right.

Thirty yards down the hall, he skidded to a stop in front of a massive metal door. He fumbled feverishly with the bunch of keys in his hand. Dusty could see beads of sweat oozing out on the man's forehead.

Cursing softly, Agent 10 tried key after key in the lock, but the big steel portal would not open. A prayer on his lips, every muscle twitching with anguish and excitement, Dusty stood helplessly by, watching him try the eighth key, the ninth, the tenth, and the—

A hoarse shout from in back of him spun Dusty around like a flash of light. There, thundering down the corridor, came a Black guard. His face was twisted with rage, and he gripped a gas-gun in each hand. From each muzzle spewed a thin stream of purple smoke.

For a split second Dusty stood frozen, then he crouched and flung his body forward along the floor of the corridor. His eyes and mouth were clamped tight. He didn't dare breathe. Then his head and shoulders crashed into a yielding body. A roar of rage filled his ears as a big hulk came tumbling down on top of him.

Lungs aching for air, he twisted sharply to the left, rolled over and scrambled to his feet. Through slitted eyes he saw the Black guard striving to squirm around on his back and bring up his gas-guns.

Dusty pressed his own gun trigger. The big hulk of a man trembled violently, then went stiff, his huge red tongue lolling out one corner of his mouth.

Lungs at the bursting point, Dusty staggered back toward Agent 10. The door was now open, and the Yank spy was beckoning frantically.

"Nice work, Ayres!" he said as Dusty reeled up to him. "You'll do! My God, man, go ahead and breathe. It's all right. Those gas-guns are only effective at close quarters. The gas in them is light and rises instantly. Come on—now we go to work!"

The air whistled out of Dusty's lungs, and for a moment everything swam crazily around in front of his eyes. But a minute later his lungs expanded normally and his vision cleared. He was still gasping for breath though as he stumbled into the room.

CHAPTER 10
HELL BLOWS UP

A T FIRST glance, Dusty had the impression that he had entered a glassware store. He could see nothing but glass funnels, glass bells and glass globes. But presently his eyes took in the details.

The room was of ordinary size except that it had an exceedingly high ceiling. Along the right wall were three rows of current meters, domed with glass. And from the bottom of each of the meters extended an inch cable which ran to a criss-cross series of glass tubes attached to the far wall. At the top of each glass tube was a big double-throw switch, at the moment in a negative position.

The left wall was a mass of relay boxes, glass battery cells, graduated rheostat controls, and current recording dials.

The ceiling, however, was the most fascinating of all. It looked like a roof of suspended, coned, spike-like objects. The tip of each cone was attached to the next by coiled strands of copper wire, spaced in such a peculiar way that it gave the impression of being a flimsy layer of copper gauze.

"Come on, Ayres, snap into it. Here, start busting those glass tubes!"

Dusty took the wrench that was thrust in his hand, went over to the rear wall and started swinging. As he broke the first tube there came a loud crack and a tiny jet of flame. It startled him for an instant and he went back a step.

"Don't worry!" came Agent 10's panting voice. "You're just shirt-circuiting minor lead-ins. Bust them all—fast!"

The Yank pilot grunted and renewed his swinging with a vengeance. Sound rang and blasted against his ear-drums, but he didn't stop until all the tubes were dangling stems of shattered glass. Then he turned to Agent 10, who was disconnecting the cable of the current meters. The man seemed to have a hundred pairs of hands, so fast did his fingers fly.

"Those rheostats!" he panted without looking up. "Swing them all to the 'Full-on' mark. Then get ready for all hell to break loose."

Ten seconds later Dusty had completed the job.

"Okay, Ayres," came the spy's voice at his side. "Now, the last thing, and God grant we're right. See those throw switches! There're ten of them. I'll start at the left you start at the right. We swing them down. But when we swing the last two, get out of here fast. I think we'll have a couple of seconds—not any more. The door is ready to jerk open. You do it, and pile out first. Set?"

Dusty nodded. Together they went over to the switches. Two, four, six, eight of them went down. Suddenly Agent 10 grabbed Dusty's wrist. But the Yank pilot also heard the pounding of footsteps along the corridor outside. He glanced at Agent 10.

"To hell with them," he blazed. "When I say three, pull and run for it! One—two—three!"

Two switches clicked down into their grooves and two frantic Yanks dived for the door. Dusty jerked it open, started out, and stumbled to a stop. Then there came a great crash of sound and he was flung flat. Through blurred eyes he saw the huddled form of Agent 10 still part way in the room. The room was a room no longer. It was a seething mass of flame.

Subconsciously, Dusty realized that the corridor lights had gone out, and that voices harsh and rasping were adding to the bedlam created by the crackling flames. And above it all was a shrill whine that rose and fell in modulated crescendo.

But only subconsciously did he realize all those things. The active part of his brain was concentrated on the huddled form of Agent 10. In some way he had fallen, and crashed his head against the steel doorjamb. A thin trickle of blood, shimmering in the light of the fire, was running from a small gash where the hair met his forehead.

Spinning over and back, Dusty scooped him up in his arms and staggered out into the dark hallway. His heart sank as he saw the faint outlines of huge bodies that blocked his path. But he didn't check his pace. Clinging to Agent 10 with one arm, he shoved the gas-gun out in front of him, squeezed the trigger grip, and charged madly forward.

What happened next he didn't know. He had the wild sensation that he was wading through a nest of boa constrictors. Hands, feet and bodies seemed to tangle about him. Screams of fear and pain vibrated against his ears. Then suddenly, he was plunging blindly forward in a sea of total darkness.

In one tiny corner of his brain was a prayer to the goddess of luck, and the realization that the Blacks in the corridor were too haywire themselves to realize that an enemy was beating his way through their struggling ranks.

AS HE BROKE THE TUBE THERE WAS A TREMENDOUS BURST OF FLAME.

Presently he was free of them, and staggering toward—God knew where. But he kept on going. Instinctive self-preservation forced him to do that. Behind him was danger. Probably ahead of him, too. But for the moment he didn't care.

He only prayed that Agent 10 had been right in his belief that they had ruined this cursed hell, and freed the air over America.

His brain playing tricks with him, Dusty went stumbling onward, crashed into walls, groped his way to the left or right, crashed into more walls, and kept on going. Then presently he became conscious of a voice in his ears and something pounding him between the shoulder blades. It was Agent 10's voice, and Agent 10's hand.

"Ayres! Ayres, for God's sake, let go! I'm okay!"

Dusty lurched to a stop, and let the spy slide off.

"Good God, man!" hissed the voice in his ear. "You're not a truck horse, and I'm all right. Just a bump. Must have fallen and walloped my head."

"You did," panted Dusty as he leaned wearily against a steel wall. "Now what? Guess we're lost, aren't we?"

"I wouldn't be surprised," came a chuckle in the darkness. "At first I thought a Black had me. Then I felt your insignia, and knew it was you. By the way, lad, thanks, plenty. I saw those Blacks just as I spilled over. I—"

"Do you think we did it?" gasped Dusty. "I mean—what you wanted to do?"

"Damned right! Hear that high hum? That's from the generators. They're running wild. Feel this wall it's even hot. Come on, Ayres, damned if I know what might happen now. We've got to find a way out. Here, take my right hand, then feel your wall with your right hand, and I'll feel my side with my left. Let me know if you touch the stairs. One of us is bound to soon. Then we'll go up. That's our only exit."

THEN BEGAN an ordeal of fear and uncertainty. Dusty lost all sense of time. From out of the darkness behind, came a jumble of shouts, curses and screams. Above it all was the eerie, high-keyed wail of powerful generators spinning themselves to destruction. A strange smell filled his nostrils and gagged him in the throat. His head felt surprisingly light and his feet, like chunks of lead. His brain swore a thousand times that he could not take another step, yet he stumbled on and on, one hand feeling the wall, the other gripping Agent 10's hand.

Eventually Agent 10 jerked him across the corridor and hissed words in his ear.

"A break for us, Ayres! Here are the stairs. I think I know where we are. Follow me up three flights, then we turn sharp to the left. There's a corridor there, and a door at the end. If I'm right, it takes us outside. Now don't let anything stop you, and for God's sake don't speak. I don't know who we may meet. Okay, here we go. Hang onto the tail of my tunic."

His leadened feet finding the first step, Dusty started stumbling upward. Higher and higher they went in the pitch darkness. Twice his heart stood still as bellowing, unseen forms charged down past them, but—the tunic he clutched kept jerking him onward and upward.

Stairs, hundreds of them, thousands—would they never stop

climbing? Suddenly, smooth steel flooring was under his feet, and he knew he was going down a corridor. Another eternity, and Agent 10 stopped abruptly. It was all Dusty could do to check himself from crashing into him.

"Right, Ayres!" came the hoarse whisper. "Hold it 'til I try these keys. Then be ready for anything—it's going to be guess-work from now on."

Metal scraped against metal. A gasping sigh from Agent 10, and the click of a bolt as it slid back.

A blast of fresh air hit Dusty in the face. It was like tonic, and his aching lungs gulped it in. But a moment later steel fingers gripped his arms, dug into the flesh so hard that he winced from the pain.

"Good God, Ayres, come over here close. Take a look through the crack!"

The steel fingers pulled him forward, and the next thing Dusty knew he was trying to focus his eyes on a blur of fantastic shadows. They spun around crazily, then slowed down, became motionless and took on definite outlines. The blood beat furiously against his temples, and his heart seemed about to explode within him.

Dusty found himself looking out into a gigantic hangar. Planes of every type and description were packed in wing to wing, every one of them jet black. The light of early dawn that seeped in from the front end enabled him to see. As he looked toward the front, he realized that the hangar was not a hangar, but a great cave with a cement floor, cut deep into the side of a hill. Beyond, he could dimly see rolling countryside that merged into the horizon in the early morning mist.

Fighting his jangling nerves, he tried desperately to study all the details of the scene. But he could only get the general panorama of it all. Planes and planes, over a hundred of them at least. A squadron of the sleek, black monoplanes which had attacked him over the Canadian border. A couple of squadrons of trim, cowled-over, high-altitude observation planes, their gas and H.E. bomb racks loaded to the hilt.

And last but not least, three squadrons of twin engine, blunt-nosed bombers. A second glance at them and he knew that they were the famous radio-controlled bombers he had heard so much about. There was no pilot's cockpit. Instead there was the small radio-shielded compartment that housed the electrical robot-pilot. And behind that were two bomb compartments, with two and one half tons of death and pestilence in each one.

As he peered at them closely, Dusty could see the row of long tubes that extended down from the underneath part of each fuselage, back near the wheel skid. The tubes slanted backward, like the stacks of a gasoline motorboat engine; and in front of the first tube was a curved, spade-shaped shield that protected the mouths of the tubes from the back-lash of propeller wash.

Germ tubes! Though he'd never seen them before, he recognized them instantly. Humaneness meant nothing to the Black Invaders. Their aim was to conquer, and they turned every weapon of destruction at their disposal against the rest of the world. But most terrible of all were those radio-controlled germ bombers. Great squadrons of them had flown over European cities, spraying the populace with invisible death. Every flesh and bone destroying germ known to medical science had been used. Those germs, coupled with the gas used by the Black Invaders, had swept everything before them.

DUSTY TURNED to Agent 10. "God—look at them—the whole side of the hill is one great drome!"

The other nodded grimly.

"Yes! It's what I suspected. They've been doing this for months, and we didn't know. The—yes, by God, I recognize that first ship—the main air fleet's here, Ayres, the main fleet! Do you get it?"

Dusty scowled, half shook his head.

"No. Just what do you mean?"

Agent 10 didn't answer immediately. He swung the door closed and pulled Dusty close to him.

"The Blacks," he began, "have been using this place as an air concentration depot, besides a communication station. One of those ships out there is the ship I was in when I left the Paris front. I recognize some of the others too—those germ bombers. Now, here's my guess. Fire-Eyes has concentrated his air force in Canada. He sent our Atlantic fleets heading for the Canal and sacrificed two of his radio-control bombers to blow that up so that the North Atlantic airways would be free for his planes. It's a cinch."

"I get you now," breathed Dusty, as the other paused. "Okay, so what next?"

Steel fingers gripped Dusty again.

"That puts it up to you, Ayres!"

"Huh? How do you mean?"

"I'm not a pilot," the Yank spy said. "But you are—the best in the business, so I hear. Now, we have just one hope. That's for you to take one of those fast ships out there, and make your getaway. When you do, you've got to definitely locate this spot. Then, hightail to Washington and give the alarm.

"If we can nail the Blacks before they get started, it won't matter what section they plan to attack. The point is, fellow, that they're here, ready, and we're the only two Yanks who know it. I can't get word through to Horner, or anybody else right now. Will you try it?"

"Hell, yes!" Dusty snorted. "Certainly I'll try it. But they'll nab you if you stick here, won't they? The Black Hawk knows you knocked him out."

"The Black Hawk isn't going to see me again," was the calm answer. "But get going, Ayres. We're wasting time now. Here's my gas-gun. Use it if you have to, and good luck. You've got one break—the hangar's empty. They must all have rushed inside to see what the hell was going on. Okay!"

The Yank pilot eased open the heavy door and slipped into the hangar. The click of the door closing behind him gave him a queer sensation. It was as though he had stepped out of one world and into another, leaving behind a brave and loyal countryman.

For a fleeting instant Dusty became possessed with a wild desire to go back in and insist that Agent 10 come with him. The two of them could make it in a pursuit ship in a pinch. If not, then take one of the observation ships. Agent 10 might be going to his doom. He wouldn't stand a chance with the Blacks any more.

The pilot half turned, started to reach for the door knob, then checked the movement, and let his hand drop to his side, as he recalled Agent 10's words, "No matter what happens, Ayres, my job is with the Black Invaders; yours with the Yanks. But, we're both working toward the same goal!"

Yes, the man was right. Their jobs were totally different, yet the goal was the same. Perhaps they would never reach it, but—There was a job to be done first.

Crouching close to the floor, in the shadow of a big oil drum, Dusty concentrated his thoughts on the task at hand. As far as he could see, in the dim light, the opening of the hangar was blocked by a row of the big gas and germ bombers. They were radio controlled, and he knew that he wouldn't stand a hope in hell of getting one of them off the ground. He had to get one of those Black Darts. He could handle that crate, all right.

A new thought came to him and his heart beat faster with eagerness. If he stole one of the Black Darts he could turn it over to the U.S. Chemical Department and let them analyze that sleep gas. Perhaps they could perfect a mask against it.

Now he started to worm his way toward the front of the hangar. He hoped fervently that he'd find one of the small black monoplanes near enough the opening so that he could wheel it out into the clear. Ahead, he could see the ground mist rising, but it was still too thick for him to form any idea of the terrain that lay beyond.

And then suddenly he froze, motionless, beside the tail of one of the gas bombers.

CHAPTER 11
THE STEEL SNAKE

OFF TO his left, Dusty had heard a door slam, and heavy footsteps were running across the floor of the hangar. They came nearer and nearer. He just barely had time to brace himself, when a lumbering guard came around the end of the plane. The Black, who was headed toward the front of the hangar, didn't see Dusty until he was practically abreast of him. And then it was too late.

With the savageness of a cornered tiger, the Yank hurled himself forward, his gas-gun held in front of him, and pressed the trigger. A faint, choking cry rang out and the Black went spinning backward, crashed into the wing of the next ship, then pitched forward face down on the floor.

At that instant panic gripped Dusty. Head down, he started zigzagging around ships toward the front of the hangar. He was but two rows from the opening when he came to a dead stop. There was the Silver Flash, right under the left wing of a big germ bomber, and nothing in front of it but God's open air.

But as he crawled forward a dozen yards, he saw something that quelled his first impulsive joy. There, standing in front of the right lower wing, was an evil-faced figure in mechanic's overalls. In one hand he held a pot of black fabric dope, and in

133

the other a fine-haired brush. Half the top surface of the right lower wing was already a glistening, jet black.

With a leap, Dusty shot forward, cursing vehemently. The Black mechanic glanced up wide-eyed, gaped at him, and then with a choked growl grabbed for his holstered gas-gun. But the Black's hands hadn't touched his gun when Dusty crashed into him, and brought his gun hand up with every ounce of his seething strength.

The Black took it square on the point of his chin and Dusty booted the guard clear of the wheels, then spun around and leaped into the cockpit.

His fingers found the fuel throttle and air compensator and rammed them forward. At the same time his right foot booted the electric-inertia starter. With his other foot he released the wheel brakes.

Split seconds snapped by, a tiny, high-keyed whine, and then the steel prop spun over. Dusty was so thrilled at being in his Silver Flash again that he didn't see the group of Black soldiers that dashed toward him. Not until the Silver Flash leaped forward, was he conscious of the big, clawing hands on the rim of his cockpit. And then he didn't care. The Silver Flash was under him once more, and he had valuable information. All hell and high water weren't going to stop him now.

Out of the hangar he raced, cleared his wheels and went streaking up into the cold, gray sky of early dawn. Hardly realizing it, he pounded his fist against the armor plated side of the fuselage.

"Now, damn you, try and stop me!"

The altimeter needle showed almost fifteen thousand. With a gasp, he jerked back the throttle to the halfway mark, and started to coast down in lazy circles. Below him, a sea of mist hid everything from view. But at the ten thousand foot mark he was able to see the ground.

At first glance it all looked like a stretch of ordinary countryside. Then gradually he came to observe the detail of the scene.

To his left there was a row of three hills, close together. A glance at his compass showed that they ran from east to west. On the south side of each hill was a wide opening. Sliding lower he saw that each opening was the entrance to a hill-hangar. In the mouth of the center hangar were several figures pulling and hauling a brace of Black Darts out into the clear.

Down Dusty went, thumbs on the electric trigger trips. As the guns spewed death he realized with a start that the last time he'd fired them they'd been jammed. The Blacks had obviously cleared them since, with the idea of using them themselves. A harsh laugh burst from his throat.

"Thanks, you rats!" he roared. "Now have some!"

THE MOUTH of the center hill-hangar had become a scene of wild panic. Black uniformed figures were crashing into each other in a frantic effort to get back out of range. Some of them took only a few steps and then went sprawling, their bodies full of made in America bullets.

Down went that mad eagle, right to the very lip of the opening. Then killing his guns, he careened up the side of the hill. At the top he winged over and started down again. But, suddenly he checked the maneuver, hauled the nose up to a forty-five degree angle, and skidded out, away toward the south. For southward he had seen something very strange.

His first impression was that he was seeing some gigantic snake, of prehistoric proportions, curving southward along the ground. Hunched forward over the stick he coasted down toward it, eyes narrowed. The front end he couldn't see. It was lost in the mist far ahead. But the rear end was blunt and glistened dully in the faint light of early dawn.

He put on a bit more speed and went forward at five thousand feet. Three minutes later he was right over the strange monster. But he was as mystified as ever. The thing looked like a dulled silver band pressed against the ground. It was about a quarter of a mile wide, and as he got closer, he thought it was striped lengthwise and horizontally.

Frowning, he slid down to a bare two thousand feet. Without warning a ribbon of jetting tongues of flame whipped up at him. Instinctively he rammed the throttle all the way forward, and cut sharply away. The Silver Flash faltered in the air and the heat of a thousand blast furnaces surrounded him.

For a moment he thought his ship was on fire. The spade grip of the stick in his hand actually heated up. And his feet resting on the rudder pedals became warm. Frantically he jerked back the glass cowling and gulped cold air into his lungs.

Choking and gasping, sweat pouring off his forehead, Dusty turned in the seat and looked down. The thing was far below, a good five miles to his right. It looked exactly as it had before, save for a thin haze of blue smoke that clung about it. He brushed his hand across his eyes, and looked down again. But the picture had not changed.

He cursed, yanked the Silver Flash around on its tail, and pointed the nose downward. The twenty-five hundred horse-power under the cowled nose bellowed in protest against the terrific speed, but he grimly held the stick jammed up against the instrument board. The air-speed needle quivered at five hundred, then slid up to five-twenty-five, to five-fifty. Prop wash swooped down over the edge of the open cowling and stung his face, but he sat like a man of stone, eyes riveted on the long, striped thing down there on the ground.

A thousand feet up, the air-speed needle was lodged fast against the 650 m.p.h. peg. The ship had ceased to be an airplane; it was a Silver Flash zipping through the air. And guiding it earthward was a crazy man who had but one idea in mind—to get close enough for one quick look at that thing which spewed fire into the air.

And then, it happened again.

From the back of the snake, a ribbon of jetting flame, shot skyward, and the sensation of heat smote Dusty again. He was racing straight for a curtain of fire. There was no turning off now. Like a meteor he went through the blast furnace and up again into cold air.

For another instant he felt as though his ship was in flames. Again the spade grip on the stick had grown hot. But it was all over in an instant. And now as the Silver Flash screamed heavenward in its zoom, Dusty sat numbed. It wasn't a snake— it was a long, strung out formation of midget flame tanks!

Midget flame tanks—one of the most destructive war weapons known to man. They were little more than heavily armored airplane fuselages without wings. No obstacle was too great for them to overcome. Like metal rats they could eat their way through any sort of defense.

In official dispatches, Dusty had read countless accounts of what the Black Invaders had done with them in Europe and Asia. They had served as escort for troop units, as scouts for the big bombardment tanks, as the advance guard for an attacking army force, and more effective still, they could transport several army corps deep into the heart of enemy-occupied areas.

Just how these midget flame tanks were constructed no one but the Black Invaders themselves knew, for one had never been captured intact. The European forces only knew the result of the attack. The tanks could shower flames on their enemies be they in the air or on the ground. Nothing, not even the best war plane built, could withstand the furious heat they threw long enough to do any destructive work at close range. High-altitude bombing by H.E. was the only course left, and as the war in Europe had proved, when the defenders did that, the Invaders simply sought the interior protection of their flame tanks, and kept right on going.

And now there were thousands of midget flame tanks down there on the ground, all lined up in formation advance positions. No wonder they looked like a big, criss-cross striped snake. Their burnished steel plating shimmered like scales in the early dawn light. Naturally they had attacked with their spouting fire when Dusty had gotten down too close. The Blacks inside of them had seen the Yank air force markings on his wings.

FOR SEVERAL moments his brain spun wildly. But eventually he got his thoughts in order, leveled the Silver Flash off its whining climb and swung south in line with the tanks. Engine wide open, he tore through the air.

At the end of five miles he ran into heavy clouds and was forced down to a ten-thousand-foot level in order to keep the ground in sight. Thus far he hadn't spotted a single place he knew. It seemed as though he were flying over an endless, rolling wilderness; each mile was but a facsimile of the one before.

Then a mile further on, he came to the front of the tank line. It was arranged in fan-shape position. He realized the reason for this immediately. Once the line got underway, the tanks would separate to the left and right, thus making a wider path of advance. That would permit greater operation ease for each individual unit, and reduce the possibility of direct hits from aircraft bombers.

Where were these demons headed? South to be sure. His compass needle told him that. But what lay south?

In time of war an airman often blesses clouds, for they afford him a haven of retreat in case things get too hot. But at the moment Dusty cursed the clouds which hung like a blanket just over his head. They cut out the light of dawn, turned objects on the ground into blurred shadows, and cut down his visibility to less than five miles ahead.

But grimly he kept on flying south. The tank line was far behind him now. Nothing but mist-covered rolling country ahead. Eventually a lake flashed by on his right. It was a small one, less than a couple of miles across. Then two more flipped past on his left. But they told him nothing as to his whereabouts.

Suddenly, without warning, hell broke out of the cloud layer and the air chattered with the savage yammer of aerial machine guns. One glance upward, and he went spinning around in a dime turn, then zoomed into the clouds. Six sleek, black monoplanes had tried to jump him.

For an instant he was filled with a desire to slide out of the clouds and give those Black pilots something to remember him by. But he curbed the idea. He had an important job to do, and so far he had gotten nowhere.

Holding the ship on a due south course, Dusty flew blind through the clouds for ten minutes, then raced down into the clear. He came out at five thousand. Directly below him was the same rolling countryside. But as he strained his eyes ahead, his heart leaped over, and he let out a wild shout.

Far ahead the clouds parted and sun was drifting through. There in the golden light was a broad expanse of water; and far to the right, on the shore, a big city, the smoke of its industries belching from myriad stacks.

Dusty didn't need to look at his roll map. He knew he was racing straight for the city of Duluth on the western tip of Lake Superior!

And as he saw his exact position, the whole situation sprang into sharp relief. Three hundred fifty miles due north from the Minnesota border line, deep in the rolling wilderness of Ontario was the hidden force of the Black Invaders. Gas and germ bombers, observation ships, countless pursuit planes, and a great five-mile column of midget flame tanks were only three hundred fifty miles from the United States border. And perhaps they were ready to start a death raid at any moment.

THOUGH DURING his talks with Agent 10 he had guessed the possibility of such a thing, the whole thing became a clear picture in his brain. No wonder the Canal had been destroyed; no wonder fake messages had sent the Central States air units flying out to the west coast. With his secret air and communication base already established in the Wilderness of Canada, Fire-Eyes had only to give the signal and his devilish forces would go crashing straight through the middle of the United States and split the country into two isolated parts.

With a muttered curse, Dusty snapped on the radio power switch and twirled the dial knob to the Washington H.Q. wave-length reading.

"Captain Ayres calling Washington H.Q.! Captain Ayres calling Washington H.Q.! Emergency... emergency... return signal at once!"

As he yelled into the transmitter tube he kept his eye glued to the red signal light. Seconds passed, then a minute, and he called again. Damn them, why didn't they call back? He had to get H.Q.—he had to get through. To go there by air would take him at least an hour and a half, and that was an hour and a half too long. Maybe the tank line commander was already starting south. With those fast midget flame tanks he could reach the border in five hours, probably less.

"Captain Ayres calling Washington H.Q. Captain Ayres calling Washington H.Q.!"

Silence greeted him. He reached out and spun the receiving dial to the Chicago air base reading, and called them. Seconds later the return call cracked in his ears.

"Chicago base, 96! What do you want?"

Dusty's hand trembled as he grabbed the transmitter tube.

"Black planes and tanks three fifty north of Duluth. Get word through to Washington H.Q. that attack is expected at any moment. I advise that your air fleets move to Duluth and concentrate for attack."

"Huh? What?" the answer snapped back. "Hey, wait a minute. I'll put Major Trainor, adjutant, on."

There came a pause, and then the earphones said, "Major Trainor on this end. Go ahead."

Frantically Dusty repeated his message, and the reply made his blood boil.

"What in hell are you talking about, Ayres? The Blacks in Canada? You're crazy. The attack will be against the East Coast, and all our planes have been dispatched there. They left yesterday. I think you'd better go back to bed and sleep it off, Captain."

"You dumbhead!" blazed the pilot. "I'm telling you the truth damn it. I was captured, taken prisoner, and I—"

He almost screamed with rage as the red light winked out, telling him that Chicago air base had switched off. Desperately he tried to get them again, and failed. Once more he tried Washington H.Q. His heart leaped as the red light winked, but it sank at what he heard. "H.Q. orders!" snapped the voice. "All planes and ground stations not already informed will keep strictly off the wave-length. Station is remaining open and clear for emergency signals from scouting squadron over Atlantic. Get off!"

"But listen—listen!" roared Dusty. "This is Captain Ayres, and—"

"I don't care who you are! Get off this wave-length at once. Don't you realize that you may jam us out on something important, you fool? Signing off."

The red light winked out again.

Cursing and shouting with rage, the Yank pounded his fist against the cockpit rim. Eventually, he cooled down and started to call Chicago corps area, but he never made it, because at that moment six sleek, black vultures appeared out of nowhere, and before he knew it they had him boxed tight as a drum.

CHAPTER 12
LIGHTNING STRIKES

FOR ONE fleeting second Dusty stared at them stupidly. Then he saw twin streams of yellowish-brown smoke begin to pour out from underneath their tails.

"You don't get me like that this time," Dusty yelled. "Not by a damn sight, you rats. I'll see you in hell first."

Like a man gone mad, he whipped the Silver Flash into a half spin, then kicked it over on wing and yanked the stick back to his stomach. The black monoplane was still going round in a lazy circle as Dusty's hail of lead caught it square amidships.

For a split second the Black Dart lurched crazily through the air. And then there came a great flash of light, a roar of sound, and the plane went down in a slithering shower of wreckage.

Unable to swerve, for fear of slamming into flying pieces, Dusty thundered straight through the trail of yellowish-brown smoke. For a second his nostrils tingled, and then cool air banished the smell. He glanced up, saw that the glass cowling was open, and laughed wildly.

If he had only known that before! As long as the glass cockpit cowling was open the prop wash blasted the fumes away before they could do any real harm. The time before he had the cowling closed. Okay, now he knew, he'd teach these rats a thing or two.

Like a demon, Dusty hurled and slammed his ship about the sky. A second Black Dart went the way of the first. And two minutes after that the count was three. Fingers jammed against the electric trigger trips, he spun and looped, triple rolled, and cursed, hoped that one of those ships held the Black Hawk.

After the fourth Black Dart went down minus his right wing, the remaining two decided not to stay any longer. As Dusty screamed up toward them, they both slammed into a wild dive, and careened up to lose themselves in a cloud bank. The last Dusty saw of them they were heading northward as fast as their thrashing propellers could take them.

Still whipped up to fighting wrath, Dusty roared after them, knowing full well that he'd nail them eventually. But at the end of five miles or so, sane reason began to seep back into his battle-mad brain, and he swung back south.

RACING OVER Port Arthur and Fort Williams, cut down the west end of Lake Superior to Duluth. The air base was on the south side of the city. As he roared over it despair filled him. There wasn't a ship on the field. For a second he hesitated, decided to land and give the alarm, then changed his mind. The one man who would listen to him was General Horner, and X34 was in Washington. Yet—Even as he spun the idea over in his mind he snatched up pad and pencil from the message box and braced the pad on his knee. A second to choose the words, and he wrote!

> Commanding Officer
> Minnesota Area.
>
> Invader tanks and planes 350 miles north of border. Concentrate all available forces for attack, and advise H.Q. Washington.
>
> > Captain Ayres
> > H.S. Group 7.

Jamming it into the metal message-carrier tube in the floorboards, he pressed the release lever and sent the colored cylinder spinning down straight for the middle of the air base field. Then he banked southeast and went tearing down the heart of Wisconsin.

Minutes later he was flashing across Chicago with a second message to the corps area commander all ready to let go. And again he groaned in despair as he circled the central air base field. Like Duluth, the field was empty of planes. Not one of

its hundred odd battle planes could he see inside the hangars or outside of them. Teeth grinding against each other helplessly, he released the message cylinder, and pointed his nose up for altitude. At thirty three thousand he got a fifty mile tail wind, leveled off, and set his directional compass dead-on for Washington.

Sucking on his oxygen tube, he snapped on radio power and twirled the station wave-length dial to H.Q. But it was no use. The instant he set the receiver dial the same rough voice cracked down on him and ordered him off. Even the emergency wavelength reading for Intelligence Department got him no results.

Washington, blind to the truth, not knowing what had happened, was concentrating every bit of attention on a suspected sea and air attack against the East Coast.

In fact, as he tried to tune in other eastern stations, it seemed that the whole country had its eyes on the Atlantic. Station after station switched him off with the brief statement that H.Q. had issued orders for eastern wave-length channels to be kept open for naval and coast defense communications. Cursing and yelling at the receiving operators, he tried desperately to get them to listen in long enough to what he had to say. But it was but a waste of his breath. They had received their own orders, and they were living up to them to the letter.

Finally, ears burning and eyeballs hot with tears of rage, he slammed off his set, gritted his teeth and cursed the Silver Flash on to greater speed.

As though it were something alive and fully conscious of the important part it was playing in a desperate mission, the plane plunged madly through strips of bad weather and fair without so much as missing a single rev.

But to Dusty the seconds were hours. And his thought didn't help any. They pictured all kinds of horrors taking place on the Minnesota border.

He saw bombers and tanks smashing the border city to flaming ruins; saw the long snake of midget flame tanks crashing and pounding down the length of Wisconsin into Illinois, to the very gates of Chicago. And nothing to stop them. A handful of soldiers here and there. Maybe a dozen planes at the most—death fodder for those bloodthirsty Blacks.

God in Heaven, what good now that he and Agent 10 had crippled the secret communication power station in Canada? Fire-Eyes and his army of devils had done their hellish work beforehand. They had static jammed a nation's broadcasting stations; issued fake orders, and sent the armies, air fleets and sea squadrons of the nation shooting off to half a dozen danger points. And all the time the madman from hell was sending his legions through the open and unprotected gate of the greatest country on the face of the globe. Splitting it in two so that later at his leisure he could hammer both isolated parts into humble submission.

"But he won't, by God!" the pilot roared wildly at his own ears. "He won't!"

He finished with a choked cry of rage, as the words mocked him fiendishly. Won't? God Almighty, what was there between heaven and hell to stop him? Nothing but one pilot tearing air toward Washington at thirty-three thousand feet. Dusty Ayres—speed ace—damned fool—block-headed sap!

After what seemed long centuries, he rammed the stick up against the instrument board and went hurtling down toward the military field at Washington, like a meteor from another world.

A quick spin, then a dime bank, a screaming sideslip, and a hair-raising fishtail finished him up right smack in front of the central hangar. Jerking of the oxygen tube, hurling back the glass cowl-slide, he leaped out and practically ran into a field orderly.

"A car, quick!" he bellowed. "The fastest you've got! Snap it up!"

The orderly gulped and gaped like a half dead fish.

"My God, you sir? Gripes, I thought that you were—"

"Don't think!" Dusty roared, grabbing him by the arm. "Come on, move, damn you! Where's a car!"

The orderly stuttered and stammered and finally got the words out.

"O-over there, sir. Behind Hangar Three. But I thought—I heard—you were dead, sir!"

The pilot didn't bother to confirm or deny the statement. His long legs moved like overheated piston rods, and he went tearing through Hangar Three and out the back.

A mechanic leaning against a long, sleek staff car suddenly found himself leaning against nothing but thin air, as a cyclone took the car right out from under him. He stumbled and grabbed for his gun.

"Hey! Halt, or I'll shoot!"

But Dusty didn't even hear him, or his shot that went wild. Motor wide open, he tore down the field road, raced around the corner, and streaked across the city to the War Department Building.

He was out and racing up the stone steps before the car had stopped rolling. A building orderly at the door put out his hand, started to speak, but only got a couple of words out before he went spinning sidewise into the guard railing.

Inside a bemedaled officer started to step into an elevator, and suddenly found himself facing the other way and the elevator door slamming shut behind him.

The human dynamo didn't stop until it slid to a halt in front of General Horner's office. There a guard blocked the way.

"One side!" Dusty snapped at him.

The other didn't move.

"You can't go in, sir. Staff meeting. No one is al—"

"I said one side!" the pilot roared.

As he spoke the pilot snapped out his hand, hooked it back of the guard's neck, and jerked hard. That left the doorway clear, and Dusty barged through into the room.

A staff general, his mouth half open to let out a word, gaped wide-eyed, then started to sputter like a missing engine.

"What the devil? You—get out of here at once. Who the devil do you think you are? I say get out, damn it!"

DUSTY SNAPPED him a salute, and ducked around the table to where General Horner was seated, pop-eyed.

The Chief of Intelligence was not the only officer knocked haywire by the whirlwind entrance of a blood and grease-smeared wild man in the uniform of the U.S. Air Force. All six of the big military and naval bugs seated about the table gasped and gurgled and glared.

But Dusty had no time for any of them save X34.

"Sir!" he blurted out hoarsely. "I've got to speak to you at once. Hell is popping loose!"

The big officer's shaggy brows twitched up and down in keeping with the motion of his lips as he rattled out harsh commands.

"Attention, damn you, Captain Ayres! What the devil do you think this is?"

Dusty's face went hard, and he leaned forward tensely.

"General!" he grated, "the Black Invaders are going to attack the border at Duluth by midget tanks and planes. Do you understand? They're in Canada, and have probably started their attack already. And we haven't got anything up there to stop them!"

The words blasted out like machine-gun fire, and created just about the same effect. Every officer at the table leaped to his feet and stared at the pilot as though he were some queer animal that had suddenly dropped down through the ceiling.

It was General Horner who first found his tongue. His face was beet-red with rage.

"By God, I'll have you court-martialed and shot!" he roared. "You failed on a trusted mission, and now you have the insolence to come back here with some crazy cock-and-bull story. Why, you young pup, we know where the attack is coming from—by sea and air, you young whippersnapper, off the East Coast!"

Tears of stark madness were close to Dusty's eyes. He put out both hands pleadingly; the gesture including them all.

"Shoot, and be damned to you all!" he raved. "But for God's sake, listen to me! I was captured, forced down, and escaped. I saw them with my own eyes—hundreds of planes twice as many midget tanks. And they are only three hundred fifty miles north of the Border. Oh, for God's sake can't you see? We've been tricked! We've—"

"Just a minute!" cut in a ranking naval officer. "You've seen them, eh? What proof have you got?"

Dusty went back a step.

"Proof?" he choked out. "My God, haven't I just told you? Proof you want? Here—here, look at that!"

He rammed his hand into his tunic pocket, jerked out the gas-gun and slapped it down on the table.

"There!" he bellowed at them. "That's one of the Black's gas-guns. A charge from that and you drop like a fly. You hear what I say? Well, I heard those very words from the lips of the Black Hawk himself!"

He grabbed the gaping General Horner by the shoulders and actually shook him.

"And do you know who gave me that?" he yelled. "Agent 10! Agent 10, do you hear? He was up there with me. He helped me escape. Damn it, we cleared the air for you. Now, for God's sake, wake up, all of you, and believe me. We've got to do something, and do it fast!"

But they all stood there like petrified clothes racks, gawking at him in complete and dumbfounded amazement. Never in any of their glorious careers had a junior officer ever clouded up and rained down upon them in such hide-blistering wrath.

At first they couldn't believe what they saw and heard, then they couldn't understand it, and finally, being men steeped in service tradition and red tape, they didn't know what to think.

Caution dumped over the side, his brain on fire with seething anguish and anxiety, Dusty tore into them, ripped them up and down, left and right, and backward and forward. The words spilled off his lips like torrents of water going over a broken dam.

He told them the whole story from beginning to end. Many details he left out, but that was only because in his excitement he forgot them. But he gave them the true picture as he knew it, and pounded the table with both fists.

And finally, throat tired, breath exhausted, he came to a hoarse, faltering stop.

"Now do with me as you wish!" he finished. "But for the love of God, believe me!"

Tight-lipped, faces pale, they looked at each other. That is, all except General Horner. He grabbed Dusty and swung him around.

"But they couldn't possibly be there, Ayres!" he got out, doubtfully. "How in the world could they have done it?"

"I don't know!" panted Dusty. "Probably came in at altitude at night. There's no one around there for miles. And their transports could bring fifty of those tanks apiece. I don't know, but I tell you they are there—*and ready!*"

"Answer me this!" snapped the other. "You say the air had been jammed. That's right. But at three o'clock this morning we got definite word from one of our Atlantic patrol squadrons that the Black fleet had been sighted. We checked back and got confirmation right away. How do you explain that?"

"Only this way, sir," said Dusty. "Agent 10 and I destroyed their power station at two. That left them only the wireless. So they ordered their fleet to proceed on a fake attack, in order that their original plans wouldn't be knocked haywire before they could carry them out."

As sudden inspiration struck the pilot, he turned to the ranking navy officer.

"Tell me, sir, where are the 2nd, 10th, 12th, 16th, and 20th Atlantic Battle Squadrons right now?"

THE ADMIRAL glared at him a second, then grabbed the inter-office signal system and barked some orders into the mouthpiece. There were a few moments of silent waiting, then the receiver crackled sound, and the admiral's face went white.

"My God!" he gasped. "Their position has just been reported off the Florida coast, proceeding back from the Canal. I—I didn't order them to the Canal!"

"See?" cried Dusty wildly. "And that's one of the fake orders I heard. It was part of their plan. They jammed your air and sent out fake orders. And the only orders that you've been able to get through were the ones you sent out after two o'clock this morning."

With a roar, General Horner leaped toward the door.

"The signal control room will tell us the answer!" he cried.

As one man they all leaped after him. That is, all except Dusty. He started, but at that moment his strength failed him. He lurched drunkenly against the corner of the table and went reeling up against the opposite wall. Only an instinctive sense of balance saved him from crashing headlong on the floor.

He felt sick, as though a thousand demons of hell were driving white-hot spears through his insides. He wanted to lie down, to throw himself headlong on the floor, and never get up again.

He'd been going through mental and physical hell since the beginning of time, it seemed, and every muscle and tissue seemed drained of its last drop of strength.

But his fighting heart wouldn't let him quit. Through? This was only the beginning. From now on it would be real war, real fighting, no playboy stuff like he'd been having. Stay on your feet, damn you, Ayres!

Mechanically his feet moved, took him to the door and through it. Then down the hall to the elevator, and eventually he found himself stumbling along the corridor toward the signal control room on the roof. He had to see it through. He just couldn't quit now.

Halfway to the door it flew open and General Horner came tearing out. At the sight of Dusty, he put on speed and raced up to him.

"You were right, son!" he snapped. "The Atlantic attack is a fake. Just a small carrier squadron drawing our ship and plane patrols south. Just received a check on it. Listen, Ayres, it's up to you, lad. You've got to do it!"

Dusty eyed him through glazed eyes.

"Do what?" he got out thickly.

"Just this," replied the other, speaking rapidly. "Get word to all western units, bombardment groups, corps areas, tank battalions, everything! They started moving toward the Mexican border on fake orders. Orders sent out two hours ago right from here. I—"

"Two hours ago?" cried Dusty.

General Horner's eyes went deadly.

"Gleason, the signal officer!" he grated. "A rat spy in our own nest, by God. I've just shot him. But not before he smashed things up. Jordon caught him contacting a Black Agent station near St. Louis. They were fighting as I came in. And the rat smashed all transmitter equipment for unit stations west. We can't depend on the phone, or waiting until Jordon gets it repaired. It's you, Ayres. Go up, and fly west. Use the emergency wave-length, and sign the War Office code number. Order all fast mobile units to the Duluth area. Get it?"

"Right, sir. I'll do it. Code number 4Z2, isn't it?"

"That's right! Now get going. I'll phone the field to have your ship ready. And pray God, H.S. Group 7 can hold things in check until reinforcements get up. It'll take four hours at least."

Dusty, who was running down the hall, skidded to a halt.

"What?" he roared. "H.S. Group 7? My own gang?"

"The only air unit we can get on the radiophone," came the quick reply. "It's still at Dayton. Air Force H.Q. is contacting Major Blake right now!"

Like a gigantic cloudburst roaring down into bone-dry reservoirs, strength and mile-a-second action whipped back into Dusty's body. That Gleason had turned out to be a traitor, had stunned him and fired him with a desire to go on serving. But the realization that his own gang was being sent to fill the breech against what he knew to be overwhelming odds was like the sounding of the death knell itself. For almost two years that rough and ready brood that composed the 7th had been everything in his life.

And now the emergency of war was sending them hurtling

down the mouth of hell. Twenty of the best against hundreds of the worst, and he couldn't join them. Not for several hours at least. And by that time, they might all be—

He finished the thought with a savage curse that jerked General Horner's eyes wide open. Then he dived into the elevator and shot downward.

CHAPTER 13
THE DEVIL'S ODDS

HIS ARRIVAL at Washington military field was simply the arrival of a second cyclone. Exactly eighteen seconds after he skidded the staff car to a stop he was in the cockpit of the Silver Flash and heeling home the throttle and air compensator.

The plane, like a horse that has just been watered and fed, streaked into the air from almost a standing start and zoomed heavenward like a rocket gone crazy.

Swinging southwest, Dusty set a semicircle course that would take him as far south as the northern tip of Alabama and as far west as the central part of Kansas. And away he went, a madman with a job to do.

Roaring full out, he raced down the borderline of Virginia and West Virginia, emergency wave-length set at the true reading.

One part of his brain directed his lips that repeated the War Department Code over and over again. And the other part of his brain struggled and suffered the hellish tortures of a thousand and one taunting thoughts.

Every few minutes he glanced at the magnetic dash watch and tried to picture in his mind what was happening to High Speed Group Number 7. Had they started? Were they on the way? Were they there and in a scrap?

Questions, like countless tongues of fire, lashed and whipped through his head. At times he felt that he was going mad. That he couldn't stand it a second longer. He had to veer north; tear up to the border and join the hell-fight with his gang. God, he couldn't bear the thought of what they might run into. They didn't know; they didn't suspect, but being Group 7 they'd tear into anything they saw.

A hundred times he reached out to twist the wave-length dial to his Group reading, and yell a warning across the miles of air space to Major Blake and the boys.

But each time that certain trait, which we call a sense of duty, forced him to pull his hand away. He couldn't lose the time for that.

His job was to call and get a check-back from a hundred other stations.

Roaring, thundering through storm clouds and brilliant sunshine, he became a mechanical man, now twisting the dial reading, now barking the War Department Code number into the transmitter tube, now twisting the dial for a receiving check-back, now yelling the emergency order to the operator listening in miles away from him.

Several times local magnetic disturbances blotted out his call or the check-back, and he was forced to change altitude, sometimes going down to within a few feet of the ground in order to get his message through.

Twice his own signal light blinked, and with a prayer on his lips that it might be orders for him to join his outfit, he switched over to receiving. But each time it was some thick-headed corps area commander demanding additional details. His reply was usually in perfect keeping with the seething tempo of his mind.

On and on, cutting corners to Alabama and Mississippi; across the river and up through Arkansas, a human dynamo on fire but chained fast to a stipulated task by training and born-to-the-cloth duty.

And then finally the end—every station contacted and every check-back complete. In his mind's eye he pictured the scene he could not see, a great wave of armed Yank forces sweeping toward the Duluth area.

Transport planes with their load of guns and men. Fast bombers with ground supplies in the extra compartments. Troop trains thundering over steel rails. Speed tank units rattling and banging over smooth roads. Staff cars, ambulances, antiaircraft motor units whipping into action.

And all headed north at maximum speed, to what? To victory, to death, to crushing defeat.

Dusty didn't try to answer the thoughts as they flashed through his brain. He was all through thinking now. Only action was left. He'd done his job; stuck to it for three long hours of agonizing hellish torment. And now he was free. He had received no other orders.

With a savage grunt he snapped off the radio power. Let the red light wink, if it did, and be damned to it. Nothing in heaven or hell or upon the earth was going to stop him now.

Get going, Silver Flash old girl! Show some real speed now. The gang's up there, and that's where we're going!

Shouting encouragement to his ship, he tore up to high altitude, got a favorable tail-wind and went rocking across the heavens.

Three times he sighted slower units laboring along underneath him, and the sight of them sent the blood snapping and ripping through his veins. Uncle Sam was on the way—tricked in the beginning and slow to start. But now the spirit of America was at fever pitch, and the might of the greatest of all nations was racing forward to meet the black hearts that would destroy her.

Finally he got his first glimpse of the fury of hell belching up from the pit of war. It wasn't much, simply a brownish smudge way down on the horizon—too far away to see anything clearly. But it was like a bolt of lightning slashed through his senses.

War was on! It had begun! The Black Invaders had started.

For an instant something snapped in his brain and he went stark raving mad. His free fist flayed the side of the cockpit. The skin of his hand split and spattered blood. But he didn't even feel the pain, for his whole body was consumed in one great flame of berserk action.

"Come on old girl—faster, faster! There it is. We're too late! No we're not. Down you go. Take it, Silver Flash, take it."

THE SHIP virtually groaned in protest as the hand of steel on the stick jammed its nose earthward. The thin wings quivered and trembled in the tornado of propwash that lashed past. Every nut, every bolt, and every bracing wire, and every square inch of chrome-dural wing covering became something alive, exerting every ounce of effort to streak downward.

A thousand other ships would have disintegrated from vibration alone, and gone showering into eternity in so many pieces. But the best aeronautical brains were in the Silver Flash, and the best pilot in the cockpit. And added to that, the true airman's god rode the wings.

Hunched over the stick, eyes narrowed to slits, Dusty sat as a carven image. Bit by bit the brownish smudge grew bigger; changed in color and became tinted with brilliant streaks of orange and yellow.

Up and up it surged like a great billowy column connecting the earth with the skies. At the peak it mushroomed out in all directions, like a gigantic umbrella that would eventually cover the entire earth and blot out the sun from a world of horror and war.

Its exact position, he couldn't place at first. It was close to the shore of Superior, that he did know, for the waters of the western tip of the lake virtually merged into its base.

But whether or not it belched up from American territory—the distance was too great.

And then he roared close enough to pick out details. The reaction was as a fist of ice pounding against his heart. At the northern outskirts of Duluth a sea of flames and dirty smoke wound its way back, far up into Canada. Part of Duluth itself was already in flames, and the waters of its waterfront rippled red in the reflection.

The heart of the city did not appear to be touched yet by the seething conflagration oozing down from the north, but several of its skyscrapers had been reduced to jagged, smoldering stumps by H.E. bombing.

But it was the streets of the city, and highways leading southward from it, that held Dusty's eyes in magnetic horror. They were jammed with struggling figures fighting each other in one wild, insane desire to get clear of the menace that had swooped down upon them from the north.

Chaos and riot ruled. People poured out of buildings and jammed the streets, only to be mowed down and churned into bleeding pulps as madmen in motor cars raced frantically for freedom.

And behind it all a great column of flame and smoke creeping closer and closer.

From a long way off Dusty heard his own voice scream commands and instructions to milling thousands who could not and never would be able to hear him. For they weren't human beings down there. Fear had changed them into savages, maniacs who had flung off centuries of civilized training, and had but one thought in what was left of their minds—to get away.

And for hours they must have been struggling, for the streets leading south were simply moving bands of jammed humanity that poured out of that raging hell like tricklets of tar weaving their way through loose sand.

On and on they came, endless, spreading out one second, stumbling and faltering the next, as those behind piled up on top of them.

Through glazed eyes Dusty stared down at them, unable to think. The horror and terror of it all had turned his brain to a blank. His hand was frozen to the stick, and the Silver Flash thundered lower and lower, straight down to its own eventual destruction, yet he didn't move a muscle. Every part of him was paralyzed by the panorama that lay spread out below him.

Never in all of his wildest nightmares had he envisioned such a scene. He lost all sense of reality. He wasn't alive, he was dead and buried deep down in the bowels of a hell that no mortal mind had ever imagined.

"Dusty, pull out of that dive, you fool!"

A tiny thin voice from thousands of miles away—the alarm of the last thread of instinct that remained unsnapped within him. His right hand shot out to the throttle, pulled it back, and his other hand eased back on the stick.

The Silver Flash bucked and sawed, then obeyed its master; swung up its nose and went screaming up and away from certain doom. Dusty searched the smoke-filled skies.

And it was then that he saw them—a twisting, spinning mass of darting shadows high overhead. Even as he sighted them his hand rammed the throttle wide open, and his other hand jerked up the nose.

Though he couldn't see markings, he knew instantly that up there his gang, H.S. Group 7, was getting its first taste of war and death.

When he was still five thousand feet below them, one of the shadows burst into a ball of flame and came hurtling downward. It swept past him in a flash, but not before he caught a glimpse of the ship and its markings.

It was a Group 7 ship!

HOW MANY more had gone before that one? He strained his eyes upward and tried to count the planes he believed American. But it was impossible. There were too many in that milling mass—too many black shadows.

A groan choked in his throat as he saw the great fleet of little Black Darts that swept across the skies like a tidal wave. There, mingled in that aerial stampede, were the rest of his gang.

Seconds later he saw them—saw his own gang. Their leader must have given a signal for they suddenly all whirled into formation and started a wedge attack on the Black fleet.

It was then he was able to count them—five—ten—fifteen! Only fifteen? But with the blow of sadness that smashed against his heart, came also a great surging wave of pride. Only twenty to begin with, but they were showing the claws of the American eagle. Outnumbered five to one, they were holding the Black vultures at bay.

But as the Yank group started its formation attack, Dusty whipped his hand to the wave-length dial.

The Blacks had "given air," but now they were circling about the charging formation and weaving a web of brownish yellow— the web of sleep gas. Unable to shoot their way through, the Blacks were falling back on their trump mystery card.

Dusty's voice screamed into the transmitter tube.

"Major Blake... Major Blake, watch that gas... it's sleep gas. All of you, slide your cowlings open... slide your cowlings open!"

The earphones crackled.

"You, Ayres? By God, welcome! Group Seven... Group Seven, did you hear that? We're being gassed... slide your cowlings open! Attack by flights on your flanks. Ready... *fly!*"

"No, no!" howled Dusty. "Spread out... spread out... break though and reverse attack!"

He was hardly conscious that he had bellowed the order. It

166

was simply the result of memory of his fight with the Black brood.

As a unit, Group 7 might not break through, even by flights. But individual attack would break the spinning cordon of Darts, and a reverse attack would tend to drive them back into their own web. And if they could do that, why—

But Dusty cut off speculation with a grunt. A Dart had cut out of the ring and was streaking down toward the city.

Eyes steady, face granite, the Yank kicked rudder and jabbed his trigger trips. Jetting flame spewed from his twin Brownings. Steel death sliced across the sky and lost itself in a jet black fuselage. The jet black turned to yellowish red, then to flaming crimson and went hurtling outward in a crazy arc.

Without giving it a single second glance, Dusty belted the stick over, flashed around and tore headlong into the ring of gas-spouting Darts.

There was no time to take aim, and no need for it either. The targets were there, waiting for his messengers of doom. And without a single thought for himself, he ripped and lashed into the whole bunch.

A sane man would never have done it, for it was no more than plain begging for death. But Dusty had stopped being sane hours ago. All he was now was a mechanical demon—a whipping, whirling, crashing machine of destruction.

The first ship that took his burst simply disappeared in a tower of light. The next went down with neither tail nor left wing. And the pilot of the third died even as he turned his eyes toward the hell-chariot that bored into him.

Perhaps it was one minute, or perhaps two, before the nerve of a murdering horde began to crack and bend. One crazy eagle they could handle, even though it be that madman in the silver plane, but his wild reckless solo attack had done something to the others, and now sixteen madmen were tearing about the sky.

Such must have been the thought of each pilot of that Black brood, for they suddenly broke their ring formation and started streaking toward the north. And in doing that they spelled death for six more of their number.

Like clay pigeons picked out of the air by the gun bursts of keen-eyed trap shooters, six Darts went whipping down in a shower of smoking metal and fabric.

The rest cut out across Lake Superior, but Group 7 swung sharper to the right and, lead by Dusty in the Silver Flash, cut around them and forced them back to the raging furnace that had once been the city of Duluth.

"Like hell you will!" roared Dusty, as he sent a straggler down without his wings. "There's more of our lads coming up, and they'll want a crack or two. So get around, damn your Black souls. Get around!"

"You're right, Ayres! Take a look to the south of us!"

The sound of Major Blake's voice in his ears made Dusty jump. Then with a shaky laugh he realized that he had not cut off his radio power. He turned in the seat and stared southward.

A shout gushed from his throat as he saw a great cavalcade of American planes clawing air toward the besieged city of Duluth. Another half hour and they, too, would be in the fray.

But as he turned forward the northern heavens became black with wings. Re-enforcements were also coming to the aid of the Dart pursuit ships. He grabbed up the transmitter tube.

"Major Blake! Radio-controlled gas and germ bombers headed this way… we can't let them through… they'll wipe out those refugees on the highway. What are your orders, sir?"

The reply came back with machine-gun fire rapidity.

"Every man pick a ship, Group 7, shoot for the engine and props… don't let a single ship past the city, no matter what you have to do. Okay, go to it!"

No matter what you have to do! Dusty groaned aloud as he glanced at the oncoming bombers. There were at least two squadrons of them. No matter what you have to do!

For a second he hesitated, licked his lower lip, then gritted his teeth so hard that his jaw bone ached.

"And here goes nothing!" he snarled.

With that he banged his throttle all the way forward and sent the Silver Flash straight into the path of the Black ships.

Forgotten were the pursuit planes. They were just a pack of yellow bellies who had quit under fire. But this new menace was something totally different. Their pilots were neither yellow nor courageous, for they weren't men of flesh and blood and bones. They were electrical robots—pilots created by the brains of scientists.

Death couldn't stop them. Nothing but complete mechanical destruction could do that—smashed engines, broken propellers and all that sort of thing. But mechanical or alive, they had to be stopped.

And so, with bodies hunched and eyes narrowed, Dusty and his pals flung themselves straight into the teeth of the science-made enemy.

CHAPTER 14
SUICIDE DIVE

TWISTING, DARTING, zooming, spinning and everything else, they hurled their planes about the sky. Thousands of steel bullets spat from the muzzles of their guns and found their finish in cowled engine metal.

First one ship went flopping down like a broken bird of gigantic proportion. Then another, and another, until ten in all had gone hurtling down to end up in bits on the shores of Superior. But far north, in Canada, the guiding brains at the control key sent the rest onward.

Out of the corner of his eye Dusty saw one speed up and slip past the blockade of Yank planes. With a curse he cut around after it. But one of his pals, who was nearer, beat him to it and went thundering down on it both guns blazing. Suddenly the guns went dead—jammed! Dusty pounded his throttle. But before he could act another Group 7 ship swerved sharply to the right and plowed head-on into the radio controlled craft.

A geyser of roaring flame spewed upward. The crumpled wreckage of the two tangled ships slashed against a second bomber and sucked it into their burning fury. And a few seconds later a third ship got in the way, to become a part of the falling world of fire and smoke.

Through tear moist eyes, Dusty watched it go zigzagging downward, and lose itself in the waters of Superior.

"High ceilings and happy landings, old man!" he murmured.

Then he hurled himself anew at the rest of the bombers. But as he did, a cry of surprise snapped from his lips. The "Controller" must have been signaled that a madman's blockade stood between the bombers and their objective, for the ships were swinging around to the west and then back to the north.

Chalk another one up for Group 7! Man or machine, that fire-eating gang of hell-benders could stop either.

But the gods of war had momentarily turned their backs upon the killer-hawks of Fire-Eyes, they were smiling proudly upon his ground legions.

A hundred or so of the midget flame tanks were already within the city limits of Duluth, and with its population either slaughtered or fleeing for their lives, there was nothing in front to stop that relentless advance of that caravan out of hell.

Swinging back toward the city, Dusty saw all this in a flash. What of it if the Blacks had been temporarily driven back in the air? The capture of ground was what won the final decision in the conflict of war.

And down there the Black Invaders were succeeding. Many of the tanks had pulled up in strategic positions, and he could just faintly see the black-uniformed figures that poured out of them and formed up in an advance infantry raid.

Blazing with rage, he raced downward and began raking the streets with his guns. But it was like a small boy shooting shell-peas at a stone wall. A blast from hell itself slashed up at him and the Silver Flash went rocketing up into the heavens.

Partially stunned, he sank back, gasping for breath. But the thing that jerked him all the way back was the chatter of Black aerial guns. Two Darts were slicing in at him, one from each side.

Even as he reached for the stick, a steel burst crashed through the cowling slide and splintered the glass to bits.

He cut back in, raked the right-hand Dart from prop to wheel tail skid. Its pilot probably never knew what hit him. And his death was enough for his flying mate; the second Dart whirled about and lost itself in a billowing pillar of smoke.

Dusty let it go. Not because he was afraid to follow it through that hell of smoke, but because Fate had suddenly dealt him a trumping-card in this mad game of death. True, it was only a card that a madman would play, but that didn't matter. What did matter, was checking the advance of the midget tank caravan into the city of Duluth.

True, Yank transports were landing and discharging their loads of guns and tank parts, in preparation for a counter attack. And Yank bombers were already showering down tons of H.E. upon the devastated streets of Duluth in an effort to check the slow but steady progress of the flame tanks.

And higher up, Yank pursuit and observation groups were beating back a savage assault of the Black air forces, and protecting the Yanks ground troops making ready for war.

BUT IT all hinged on time, and time was favoring the Black Invaders. Let their tanks once get complete control of the city and they would be able to protect themselves against counter air and ground attacks.

In fact, they had virtually succeeded already. From the tunneled spouts atop each tank great fountains of flame and smoke poured out, hiding their movements from all directions. Yank bombers were flying blind, and dropping their H.E. eggs on hidden targets, not knowing whether they were hitting the foe, or their own countrymen.

No, those devils could not be stopped that way. They had to be split apart; the advance cut off from the rear guard.

Dusty laughed wildly as he bellowed the words:

"And the damned thing's a one man job! My job—because the other lads haven't spotted it yet!"

It was true. Too occupied with their respective jobs, no other Yank pilot had seemingly noticed the half-mile square patch of ground, just north of the city, that the Black tanks were avoiding.

And well they should, for the section was covered with rows of giant fuel storage tanks. Millions and millions of gallons of valuable gasoline, benzene, and machine oil. To an invading army, that had penetrated far from its own base of supplies the capture of such a prize would be as a manna from the gods of war.

And it was obvious that the commander of the Black tank forces realized that, for though the storage park lay directly in the path of their advance, the tank line had split, going around the place and then converging again in a solid column a mile beyond.

Yes, that storage park offered the one chance to check the Black advance.

Sliding down a few thousand feet, Dusty studied the layout, selected the most vital spot in the storage tank area. In a moment he spotted it—a group of huge benzene tanks a bit to the left of the center.

With a nod of satisfaction, he eased open the throttle and "lifted" the Silver Flash up to fifteen thousand feet.

All about him planes were racing and tearing about, spitting streams of death from their cowled guns. And far to the south, heavy Yank guns were hammering steel into the city in a frantic effort to build up a wall of ruins that might check the tank advance until American tank corps could be assembled.

For a moment he floated lazily about at fifteen thousand, while he adjusted the four armor piercing bombs with which his ship was equipped. They were only fifteen pounders, and were primarily designed for aerial attack on armored machine-gun redouts. But now he was going to use them for something different.

With steady hands he turned the timing knobs to zero, released the locking pins that held the directional fins in place, and then slipped them into the trap tubes that slanted forward through the flooring of the cockpit.

A split second later he nosed the Silver Flash over the "hump" and sent it roaring hell for leather toward the ground.

As though the Blacks on the ground had suddenly suspected the idea of his thundering plunge, a hail of steel whipped up at him. But he did not veer an inch one way or the other. A

madman going to his doom, he tore down over the city like a rocket sent from Mars.

Down, down he went, the twenty-five hundred horses under the nose screaming in wild protest.

The storage park swept up toward him. The rows of fuel tanks, looking like black pin heads at the start of the dive, grew bigger

and bigger, their round tops becoming as so many black dinner plates turned upside down.

And then, the split second of doom arrived.

A RIGID grip on the stick with one hand, Dusty shot out the other, hooked his fingers about the four spring bomb toggles and jerked upward. At the same instant he hauled back the stick with every ounce of his strength. The Silver Flash virtually screamed aloud, as it went tearing and thrashing upward.

Eyes closed, lips set in a grim line, Dusty sat frozen in the seat. Yet, it was but a matter of seconds before the world split apart and the unleashed raging fury of a thousand hells blasted up into the heavens.

A gigantic unseen hand of terrific force grabbed the Silver Flash and hurled it spinning off into space. Weakly Dusty tried to get it under control, but it was useless. Ten thousand sledge-hammers were pounding him down into the seat, and balls of fire were racing around in his brain. Touch, smell, sight, all his senses vanished. He became as nothing that was whizzing into a great void.

On and on and on into nowhere he roared, totally helpless; unable to move a muscle or even flick up his eyelids. A thousand eternities came and went. A thousand eternities filled with crashing thunder and sizzling, flashing light.

And then, life seeped back into his body, and instinct took up the job that a dulled, stunned brain was unable to cope with yet. The mad shimming stopped and the Silver Flash leveled off and raced forward on an even keel.

His eyelids parted and he looked out again on the world. He

found himself staring at thin air. With an effort, he turned his head and looked stupidly downward. Below was a vast expanse of rolling water.

It meant nothing to his aching brain at first. And then, presently as he unconsciously banked the Silver Flash around in a lopsided turn, he saw, and realized. He was high in the air and far out over Lake Superior. But he wasted no more than a glance at the lake.

Breathlessly he looked in-shore toward Duluth.

"My God!"

A gigantic fountain of boiling fire was spouting heavenward and then sloshing down again like a great canopy. The ground itself had changed into an ocean of liquid flame that spread outward in all directions. And it enveloped the center sections of the Black tank advance like a blanket of doom.

Unable to swerve aside, column after column of them were, mushing into it, like the rats of the Pied Piper rushing into the river's water. On they came, those in the rear banging and charging against those in front.

In spite of himself, Dusty groaned with the horror of it all. The Blacks, devils that they might be, did not have a chance. Tank after tank lurched to a stop and its occupants spilled out and tried frantically to scramble to safety.

But like the tentacles of an octopus, the fingers of boiling flame reached out and consumed them in the agonies of hell.

And the tanks already in the city were striving to swing around, get clear of the flames, and contact their split ranks. But Yank gunners were pounding them into hiding.

As Dusty glanced to the south he saw a column of mopping-up tanks, of the Yank army, lumbering menacingly into the city.

A job done—and he was still alive!

"But you are, you lucky bum!" he howled joyously. "You are alive—"

The rest froze on his lips, as the earphones crackled.

"But not for long, Captain Ayres!"

CHAPTER 15
BLACK PATROL

DUSTY WHIRLED in the seat. Thirty yards back of him was a sleek Black Dart. He could not see its pilot, but the voice in his earphones told him enough. The Black Hawk had him in a cold-meat shot position.

Dusty's hand on the stick started to move it, then he checked himself. If only he could gain a few seconds. Just a few, and he might catch this tongue-wagging conceited rat off guard.

"Well?" he grated into the mouthpiece. "You win this one, anyway. So go ahead and shoot, damn you!"

As he spoke he let his body slump down into the cockpit. With luck, the other's first burst might miss him, and smash into the instrument board.

"Of course I win!" came the harsh words. "You're a very clever man, Captain Ayres, but not clever enough. Oh, yes, I admit that you have hindered our progress for the time. But there is always a tomorrow. A tomorrow when you won't be there, Captain Ayres. And now, fly north, Captain. We are going back!"

The voice stopped. Dusty started to speak again but checked himself. It was now or never. He started to veer the Silver Flash slowly around to the north. But when he was halfway; he slammed down on opposite rudder with all his might, and banged the stick over.

A savage yammer of guns blasted out from behind, and hissing messengers of death zipped past his head and transformed the instrument board into a shambles.

But a split second later the hail of steel was pounding against his left wing-tips, then off it slid into thin air. He kicked the Silver Flash around in a pin-point split-arc.

"Now, damn your soul!" he bellowed. "We'll see who the hell is going back!"

But the Black Hawk didn't wait. The Dart spun over and down, then swung northward at top speed. Dusty laughed harshly, belted his stick forward and dived.

The Black Hawk must have looked back and seen him coming, for the monoplane started zigzagging crazily. The defense maneuver brought a crooked smile of scorn to Dusty's lips. With cold deliberation he squinted an eye to his telescopic sight and jabbed the trigger trips.

The Brownings barked and the monoplane seemed to cartwheel over. The Brownings barked again, and the monoplane went careening crazily off to the left. Then suddenly it spun completely over on its back, hovered in mid-air for a split second, and whipped downward straight into the boiling sea of flame.

Dusty didn't watch the horrible end. He had seen enough horror for one day.

The thing for him to do was to land. To get down near that infantry area south of the city. He was hungry. Hell, when did he eat last, anyway? And, sleep? Boy, could he cut himself a big slice of shut-eye just about now? And how! He'd contact Group 7, and breeze back to them later.

Sure, he'd land. His job for the time being was finished. To his left there, the Yank troops were starting a mop-up of Duluth. What remained of the Black tank column was rushing northward as Yank planes rained down more hell on it.

The Black Hawk was dead! And Fire-Eyes had been taught a lesson!

HE FLEW southward, circled the infantry air contact field a couple of times, and then slid down to a landing. A squad of doughboys helped him leg out. One of them gave him a cigarette. He was in the act of lighting it, when a corporal ran up.

"Captain Ayres?"

"Right," he nodded wearily.

"You're wanted over at the temporary area H.Q., sir," said the corporal, pointing. "Over in that portable shack, sir."

Dusty shrugged resignedly. God, would the big bugs never stop sending for him? He walked with heavy steps over to the portable H.Q. shack.

Inside, he pulled up short, eyes wide. The big figure of General Horner confronted him. The man stood straddle-legged, hands clasped behind him, and there was fire in his eyes.

"Well, Captain Ayres!" he boomed. "Do you think that a

junior officer can cuss and bawl out an executive war council of the ranking officers of the United States Armed Forces? Gentlemen who were captains long before you were born? Why, you deserve to be shot every day at sunrise for a week!"

The thick lips snapped shut, and the steely eyes burned into Dusty's face.

The pilot swallowed hard.

"I—I'm sorry, sir," he began. "I—"

But General Horner was shaking with laughter.

"Don't be a fool, Ayres!" he roared. "Don't spoil it by trying to apologize. It was perfect! Never seen the like of it in all my forty-three years in the service.

"I sent for you, Ayres," he went on gently, "so that I might have the honor of being the first to express the everlasting gratitude of our country for what you have done. Every report I've received has been full of your feats. There aren't words to express it. By all the laws of war and mankind you should be dead. But—well, I can only call it a great miracle. A miracle of courage and valor."

Dusty smiled.

"Thank you, General. I'm glad I did my duty, and that I was lucky. But I wasn't the only one. Everyone did his full share. And—and Agent 10, sir—he deserves far more credit than I. If it hadn't been for him, why—"

"That's what I wanted to speak about," cut in the general huskily. "He's been able to get word through to me, gave me a report on all that happened. Well, Ayres, your country owes you a great debt of gratitude and thanks. But I owe you even more than that. You did me a great service, Captain Ayres."

Dusty frowned at him.

"I don't understand, sir," he faltered.

"A secret, Ayres," said the other slowly. "Something I should not tell. But I know I have your confidence and loyalty. Agent 10 is my son."

The pilot stiffened, then looked him straight in the eye.

"And a great son, sir!" he said. "A son you can always be proud of. I shall always remember him, and pray that we will meet again."

A shadow flitted across General Horner's heavy face.

"Who is there to say that you will or will not," he murmured thickly. "Your jobs are different, but no man can foretell when your paths may cross again, or if they will. Today we gave the Black Invaders a taste of their own medicine. Perhaps that will teach a lesson to this Fire-Eyes, their leader. But with men like you, Ayres, and my son, and ten million others, this country need have no fears of the ultimate outcome of it all. Let us shake hands on that, Captain."

They clasped hands and smiled. But only with their lips did they smile, for in their eyes was the same haunting question—what would be the next move of Fire-Eyes and his devastating horde?

POPULAR PUBLICATIONS
HERO PULPS

LOOK FOR MORE SOON!

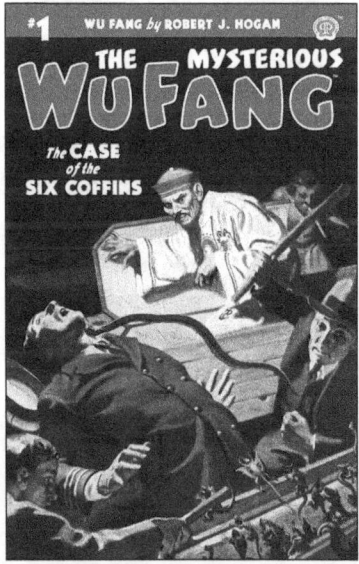

ALTUS PRESS · THE NAME IN PULP PUBLICATIONS

www.ingramcontent.com/pod-product-compliance
Lightning Source LLC
Chambersburg PA
CBHW060940180626
46817CB00004B/1639